"Behold 7 wonder stories, each structured upon a skeleton of geographic and historic truths, made flesh by their able and tender physician/writer and gifted breath by the pure power of his imagination - together forming a kind of benevolent Golem to snuggle up to each night. Bravo!"

   — Rebecca Alban Hoffberger, Founder/Director
      American Visionary Art Museum

"In seven delightfully whimsical 'fabrications,' Stang reimagines the history of people and places around the Gunpowder River—a beautiful inlet that meanders its way from North of Baltimore, Maryland, down to the Chesapeake Bay. Playful and surreal, the author takes the reader on journeys through relationships, both historical and contrived, and brings to life a rich landscape that he populates with lovers, ghosts and even a magical, sagacious fish. The Monster of the Gunpowder River is very much like the actual river it was inspired by: vibrant and fast-moving, after a flooding rain."

   — ellen cherry, Emmy-nominated Song & Story
      Alchemist

"These seven stories all share one thing in common: Each one contains at least a bit of magic, of the unexpected. Among them: a talking fish, travels back and forth in time, an underwater world, a fish-spotting dog, a man in a can, a dead man revived as a kind of human-plant, and lots of fishing. There's humor, slyness, sadness, irony, all told with wit and generosity, with deftness and grace. Stang's playwriting experience shines in these stories through fine dialogue and a strong sense of place in each tale. Above all, these tales possess a playful imagination at work."

— Phil M. Cohen, author of *Nick Bones Underground*, Jewish Book Council award for Debut Novel

"Michael Stang's magic-carpet stories fly us beyond the bounds of the real, into a world similar to this one but more magical, more coherent, and much kinder. Take the trip. A visit will do you good."

— William deBuys, Pulitzer finalist and author of *The Trail to Kanjiroba*

"The stories in *The Monster of the Gunpowder River and Other Fabrications* are a moving and elegant display of Dr. Stang's abilities as a chronicler of history, place, character, and the nuances of time on the subjects on which he chooses to turn his knowledgeable gaze—in this case, the surrounds of the Gunpowder River in Baltimore County. The pieces bring to life real symbols, icons, and landmarks filtered through the author's vivid imagination, at times melancholic and wistful, other times bawdy and outrageous. His tales are a balm for our current, challenging times."

— Dr. Hortense Gerardo, playwright, screenwriter, and Director of the Anthropology, Performance, and Technology (APT) Program at the Jacobs School of Engineering at the University of California, San Diego

"Michael Stang isn't fooling when he deems the seven stories in his first collection, *The Monster of the Gunpowder River* "fabrications." Although his sensibility is contemporary,

Stang manages, with a genial, compassionate heart and a fine sense of detail, to resuscitate a nearly forgotten genre—the tall tale, as practiced by Poe, Twain, and John Collier. Linking these stories is Maryland's Gunpowder River, and Stang's imaginative expansion of historical fact, which lead the reader to suspect that every acre of land and stretch of water in their vicinity is chock full of mysteries and meanings, only waiting to be uncovered. It's a dazzling debut."

> —James Magruder, author of *Vamp Until Ready* and
> Outer Critics Circle Nominee, *Head Over Heels*

"Written during pandemic isolation, Michael Stang's masterful collection reminds us of just how deeply interconnected we all are, barrier of time, space or species be damned! Take this slim volume with you to your favorite spot in nature and savor every page til the sun goes down. These stories will bring you back to yourself just when you most need it."

> — Roland Tec, President, PinkPlot Productions.
> Writer, director and producer of film and theatre.
> Faculty, Dramatists Guild Institute

The Monster of the Gunpowder River

The Monster of the Gunpowder River

And Other Fabrications

7 Stories by
Michael Stang

Apprentice House Press
Loyola University Maryland

First Edition

Casebound ISBN: 978-1-62720-398-2
Paperback ISBN: 978-1-62720-399-9
Ebook ISBN: 978-1-62720-400-2

Printed in the United States of America

Design by Adara Kellogg
Edited by Tyler Zorn
Promotion plan by Ava Therien

Published by Apprentice House Press

Apprentice House Press
Loyola University Maryland
4501 N. Charles Street
Baltimore, MD 21210
410.617.5265
www.ApprenticeHouse.com
info@ApprenticeHouse.com

To C. Fraser Smith (1938-2021)
Consummate journalist, author, writing partner and friend

Contents

Introduction

Why the Gunpowder River?

The Gunpowder River and North Baltimore County have been an important part of my world for many years.

I boat on Loch Raven Reservoir, I fly fish on the Gunpowder River, and my wife and I ride bikes on the NCR Trail that accompanies the Gunpowder for large stretches of its course.

The idea for this book was pre-Covid. The writing became my Covid project.

The stories are fiction, although many are populated with real people, places, and events.

The NCR Trail, also called the Torrey Brown Trail, is the trackbed of what was a section of the North Central Railroad. One who rides or walks north from the southern end of the trail will come upon the remains of one of Baltimore County's once-ubiquitous lime kilns (I gave the fictional name of "The Ferguson Lime Kiln" for the last story). Further up the trail, just north of the Glencoe stop, you will see a train signal from the 1930s. This became part of one story.

The beautiful Loch Raven Reservoir, a recreational lake and the main source of drinking water for Baltimore, expanded into its current form with the flooding of the mill towns of Warren and Bosley in 1922. Nearby Phoenix suffered collateral damage. Before the inundation, these towns were a thriving part of the area's huge cotton manufacturing enterprise that, at its peak, produced 70% of the *world's* cotton duck.

The Oldfields School is a lovely private school founded in 1867. Its most famous alumna, Wallis Warfield—who later became The Duchess of Windsor— attended from 1914 to 1916.

The Poplar Methodist Protestant Church and its cemetery as well as the Bazil AME Church exist today.

Great Feathers is the real fly shop I go to for supplies and advice. The Filling Station down the road is a great little spot for coffee and eats.

Natty Boh and The Little Utz Girl are icons that may not be familiar to those living outside the area. We are blessed these days with access to information and have only to ask our smartphones or iPads for details.

I hope you will enjoy reading these stories as much as I enjoyed writing them.

— Michael Stang

The Monster of the Gunpowder River

It was late September when I caught the monster.

Fishing that day was an afterthought. I was heading west on Mount Carmel Road and decided to make a right on Masemore. The Gunpowder River was clear with good flow.

The rod was an old piece of junk that was as much a part of my trunk as the spare tire. Having left my *car* fly box at home, I managed to find a tattered and dusty green Woolly Bugger deep under the back seat. I put on my wading boots, walked upstream along the trail then waded in.

The fish took the old fly on a downstream cast even before it swung across with the current. I eased his front half into my net after a fight that seemed more symbolic than real. His back half hung uncomfortably over the rim the way my belly hung over my belt. Quickly, I lowered the net into the water and kept it under him so the rim wouldn't rub.

He was at least two feet long and weighed twenty pounds, if not an ounce. I think we were both surprised that neither rod nor line snapped.

I could only say with certainty that he was a trout.

He wasn't a Rainbow, a Brown, a Golden, or a Brookie. Instead, he was brownish-green with nondescript circular and wormy spots and a slightly forked tail. If anything, he resembled a Lake Trout, which I had only seen in pictures. His fins were notched and tattered, and the up-facing eye was as opaque as milk glass.

Memories are slippery things, but it was one of solid stuff that flashed into my consciousness. Old Tom Spooner, who passed away three years ago, had been a fixture at Great Feathers Fly Shop. He told me—and anyone who would listen—of a monster trout he had caught on the south side of Bluemount Road the year prior. It was the largest trout he had ever seen, and he was a man who had fished three continents. He guessed thirty inches and twenty pounds, but when pressed about the species, he shrugged and said, "Never seen one like this." And when asked why he didn't keep it—it had not been caught in a catch-and-release area—he said, after a long embarrassing silence, that the fish had asked to be freed. *Yes! He asked to be freed!* "I know it sounds crazy, but me and him had ourselves a little conversation, and that's what happened. I guess I was kinda shocked by the whole thing, so I just let him go without givin' it a second thought."

People would say, "You know Tom. Half of his fish stories are outright lies, and the other half shouldn't be believed."

Tom had fished his entire life, and I could believe that he had developed a *certain* kinship with nature, but this was hard for any of us to swallow. We all feared Tom was losing it.

What did happen, though, was since the talking-fish incident, Tom, already a good fisherman, became a great fisherman—the greatest fisherman on the Gunpowder—ever.

As he was already in his eighties and becoming frailer, the boys at the shop just let the story fade. By the time of his death, Tom was no longer Tom the Fish Whisperer, he was Tom Spooner, the area's best fisher-man—and great guy.

When my attention returned, I saw that my fly was near the corner of the fish's jaw. His mouth was thoroughly nicked and scarred, and there was the rusted stub of an old hook next to mine. I kneeled in the gravelly bottom to get a closer look at my prize. As my bad knee pressed against a sharp edge of a rock, I let out an expletive and quickly found a smoother rock to kneel on. Immediately, there came from the fish's mouth a stream of bubbles and a low-pitched rumble in which I thought I heard, "Free me. Please." I looked around. No one. I looked down at him. His body twitched, and again came the same bubbles, the same sound, the same words. This time the words were unmistakable: "Free me. Please."

I took a quick accounting of myself. I'd had enough sleep. I'd had no alcohol. I had no history of mental illness. I did not feel stressed. My work as an insurance adjuster had been boringly uneventful. My wife of nearly forty years had of late been pretty happy with me. But no animal, not even my faithful Black Lab Tyson, had spoken to me, at least not in English.

"Please, mister." I saw the bubbles trail off into the current.

I looked around again, more carefully this time. Still no one. I leaned down and asked in a half-whisper, "Why should I free you?"

"I want to live," he said.

With this, I turned him upstream and submerged him briefly to let the water flow into his gaping mouth and over his gills. Then, I brought him back to the surface.

"Thank you for that, friend," he gurgled.

"Friend?" I asked.

"Yes."

"OK. We're friends. So, why do you care about living… friend?"

"Look up."

As I looked up, I tightened my grip. It's bad enough to fall prey to the old *look up trick* when done by humans, but to be tricked in this manner by a trout—I couldn't let that happen. I scanned the trees and skies above me, then turned to the fish.

"What do you see?" he asked.

"The usual."

"What is that—the usual?"

"Branches, leaves, sky—what you'd expect."

"Of course, what I see through my one good eye is different but no less spectacular. More the reflections, shifting lights, colors—all depending on the time of day and the weather."

"And the clarity of the water," I added.

"Yes. Clarity. Important."

I submerged him for longer this time and looked up again without tightening my grip. Yes, there was more to it than branches, leaves, and sky. The light filtering through the fluttering leaves became the glimmer on the riffles. I saw the birds returning to their nests and the movement of wispy clouds in a perfect blue sky.

As I brought him up to the surface, he was calm. He turned his head towards me, and I could see that his *good* eye was as limpid as the stream.

I reached back, found my forceps, and carefully removed my fly.

"Do you want me to remove the other one?"

"Please, friend. It refused to go away like the others."

He held still as I worked the rusty iron nub from his mouth.

"I'm sorry if that hurt," I said.

"Thank you for all you've done, friend," he said. "Tell me. Is this where you usually come?"

"Not usually. I was in my car and had some extra time."

"So, our meeting was fortuitous."

"Yes."

"Can you come to this place every other week at sunrise?"

"I suppose. Why?"

"To talk, of course. When you arrive, tap on the large leaning rock behind you."

I turned around and saw the rock. It was different from the others, leaning precariously over the water.

"How many times?" I asked.

"What do you mean?"

"How many times should I strike the rock? And what do I strike it with?"

He squirmed a bit. I didn't know if he wanted to be submerged again or if it was a laugh. I submerged him. When I brought him up, he immediately said, "You humans are alike, you know. Two others asked the same questions."

"Was one of them named Tom?"

"Yes. And there was another."

"I don't think it's such an unreasonable question," I said.

"What does reason have to do with it? I usually stay in that pool just beneath that rock."

"The leaning one?"

"Yes. The pool is quite deep, and the rock is very big. It goes most of the way to the bottom. If you tap with something hard—"

"Like another rock."

"Yes—like another rock—I will hear you whether you tap once or ten times. Then I will come up to meet you. Please submerge me."

When I brought him back up, I said, "And we will talk."

"Yes."

"About what?" I asked.

"The other fishermen wanted to know what the fish were eating."

"That would be helpful."

"And where they were congregating."

"That would be wonderful," I added.

"And if they were attracted to certain colors that day. Things like that."

"Do you speak to the other fish?"

"No. They don't speak, but I observe. I do wish there could be more interaction."

"Why don't you reach out to them?" I asked.

"I don't think they're interested."

"Why?"

"Because I tend to eat them—depending on their size, of course."

What kind of comeback does one have to a truth of nature like that?

"In two weeks," I said.

A few bubbles rushed from his newly-unencumbered mouth. I lowered him into the water and released him. He swam methodically into the deeper water to my right and descended out of sight. Quickly putting on my polarizing sunglasses, I could just make out his notched dorsal fin before it vanished.

At that very moment, a swarm of questions came to me. I found a pencil stub and a scrap of paper and began writing furiously. I have learned that if they're not

7 • Michael Stang

written down, thoughts will disappear as quickly as they come.

Satisfied that I had scribbled down most of my questions, I stuffed the pencil and paper into my pocket, put on my sunglasses, and took a final look towards the pool. Only the wavy darkening green to black remained.

As I returned to my car, I resolved to tell no one. I gathered a handful of rocks and made a little pile at the far end of the pull-off, something no one would see unless they were looking for it. Then, I headed home. The first chance I had, I entered the following ten two-week dates into my pocket calendar and looked up the time of the sunrise for each. I recopied in ink my scribbled questions onto an index card.

I returned to the spot twice more to be sure I could find it, looking around for landmarks that would be visible in the dark. I checked my pocket calendar daily to ensure I wouldn't miss the date. As the days went by, the excitement was slowly being replaced by worry. A talking fish? Was I losing it? Did this whole thing really happen?

Exactly two weeks later, I got up early and told my wife I was going fishing. She mumbled, "OK. Be careful." She went back to sleep.

Sunrise was at 7:04. I got to the parking area by 6:49 and put on my wading boots. Then I checked my shirt pocket to make sure I had the index card and pen. They were there.

At 7:00 sharp, I turned on the flashlight and left the

car. I located a softball-sized stone, big enough to allow a firm strike while not smashing my fingers. I made my way to the leaning rock, getting there as the morning sun turned the overhead leaves to stained glass. I checked my watch. 7:02. I took a seat on the rock, my feet in the stream.

Suddenly, I was uneasy. What if he doesn't show up? What if the whole thing was a joke? What if I was being played only to set him free? What if the entire event was in my mind? I shook my head. I'm here. I'm following through with this, whatever it is. And, if he doesn't show, what have I lost? I looked at my watch. 7:04.

I rapped the big rock once. Was that hard enough to be heard maybe fifteen feet below? I rapped harder this time, and the stone fell apart in my hand. I froze and then began looking around for another rock; that's when I saw the fish slowly making its way upward. I was relieved to see his head break the water.

"Good morning," he said.

"Good morning."

"I see you're on time. Sunrise."

"Yes."

"What would you like to talk about?" he asked.

"Yes. Yes. I have a list of questions for you," I said as I fumbled in my pocket.

The fish briefly turned upstream, dunked his head, and then resurfaced, facing me with his good eye. I found my reading glasses and looked at the card.

"Number 1. What species are you?"

"I don't know. I am different from the rest. I know that."

"Is that a problem for you—being different?"

"No."

"OK. Number 2. How old are you?

"I don't know."

"Number 3. Do you have a name?"

"Fish normally don't have names. I was given a name by Tom. Moby Penis."

A laugh shot out of me. At first, I pictured Tom Spooner laughing at his own joke. But Tom was a one-way joker. He liked playing jokes on others but was a poor sport when he was the target. He just couldn't help taking advantage of this exceptional animal. Shame on him!

Moby interrupted my thoughts. "That was his reaction when he came up with that name," he said matter-of-factly. "I don't understand the outpouring of sound that accompanies my name. It seems like an acceptable name. I do like the sound of it. Mo-by Pe-nis. You humans have two names, right?"

"Yes," I said, no longer finding humor in the situation.

"After a while, Tom called me Moby P. and later just Moby."

"And you called him Tom?"

"Yes. I would suggest you call me Moby. What should I call you?"

"My name is Robert Stanton, but you can call me

Bob."

"Not Rob?"

"No, Bob."

"Bob… Were there other questions?"

"Yes." I repositioned my readers and referred back to the card. "Number 4. How did you learn to speak?"

"I don't know. I've heard human sounds coming from above me my whole life. But the speaking just happened one day."

I'm sure he saw me furrow my brow.

"That's all I can say on the matter. Was there another question?"

"Number 5. How do you know the names of the insects?"

"Brian and Tom taught me the names."

"Brian was the first human you met?"

"Yes. Brian Jonas."

I knew Brian. Everyone did. Excellent fly tier. Like Tom, he became a more successful fisherman late in life. Maybe I was on the verge of following in their footsteps. To date, my talents would be referred to as *respectable*.

"You know, both Brian and Tom have passed away," I said.

"That's what I thought. They stopped coming."

He submerged once more.

"More questions, Bob?"

I looked down at the card. There were no more, but I wasn't ready to end the session.

"Which insects—?"

"Are we eating these days?" he asked.

"Yes."

"Up this way, it's Baetis. Lots of Baetis."

"Thanks. But tell me, Moby, why Baetis? Is it the taste?"

"Neither human ever asked me that—and they asked me a lot of questions. What is taste, Bob?"

"When we put something in our mouths—unless it's something without taste like plastic or rubber or metal or glass—we taste it... Ummm..." I looked down at Moby; he was observing me.

"Many things—especially food—when they touch the tongue...This is the tongue." I stuck out my tongue as far as I could and pointed at it. "When that happens, we get a sensation like sweet or sour or salty or peppery or other things like that."

Moby submerged for a moment and, upon surfacing, asked, "Is this taste a good thing?"

"Oh yes. Most often, it is. It usually makes our food very enjoyable."

"I'm not sure I understand taste. We eat our food because, if we don't, we get very tired and die."

"So you don't have a preference for certain insects?"

"Big ones. I like big ones. I like frogs too. And fish."

"And you can tell the difference between a real insect—"

He completed, "And the ones the fishermen tie to a hook?"

"Yes. Over the years, it has gotten easier. But when I

was young, I was caught a few times."

"And what happened? Did you speak to the fishermen?"

"That was before I was able to speak. For some reason, they released me."

"You were probably in a catch-and-release area."

He said nothing and dipped underwater for a few moments.

I continued, "These are parts of the stream where fishermen are not allowed to keep the fish."

"So there are safe areas for fish?"

"Yes."

"That is very important information! Tell me, Bob. Did you catch me in such a safe area?"

"Yes."

"So you *had* to let me go."

"Yes."

He swam upstream twenty yards and then slowly came back. He surfaced, looked at me, and repeated the same route before returning and emerging again.

"You said you *had* to let me go."

"Yes."

"Tell me, Bob. Would you have let me go if it wasn't a safe area?"

"Yes."

"Why?"

"You asked me to let you live, and you convinced me that you appreciated life."

"Thank you, Bob, friend."

"Besides, your meat is probably very tough." As I laughed, he ducked under, and when I saw him again, he was swimming in a tight circle thirty yards downstream. Fifteen minutes later, he disappeared.

I sat and waited. I removed my readers and put on my sunglasses to scan as much of the stream as possible. Nothing. Could a fish be that sensitive? Didn't he know I was joking? I guess being eaten by a friend is not funny. Or was it just the sound of the laugh that was bothering him, like with his name?

I must have waited for more than an hour. As I was beginning to leave, I heard the guttural rasping of another car pulling off the road. The door shut, and a young man came up to me, smiling. "Any luck in that pool today?" he asked before seeing that I had no fishing equipment except waders.

"No. I just came by to have a look. I used to come to this spot a lot, but I don't think there have been fish here for over a year. If you want my advice, you're better off farther upstream."

"Thanks. I appreciate that." And he left.

I put on my sunglasses again and had one more look. Then I left.

Over the next two weeks, I thought a lot about Moby. I read all my trout books and Googled more. The trout has a brain the size of a pea, and most of it is not the thinking part but the part that performs automatic functions. Given that Moby's brain, due to his size, may be equivalent to a lima bean, it still didn't explain his speech, intellect, and emotions. I was also saddened to think he wouldn't want to see me again. Some people hold grudges forever. Who could predict what fish would do? I could only hope there wasn't enough room in his lima-bean brain for grudges.

The day of our next meeting came quickly. This time would be different; I would bring a gift as a peace. offering and ply him with serious fishing questions.

I made my way to the rock carrying a large box, bringing a hammer to make sure I would get his attention. Taking a seat on the rock, I dipped my wading boots into the cool dark current. When I struck the rock with the hammer, there was a spark. I felt a sharp pain on my upper thigh and realized it had burned a hole through my thin pants. I swatted it a few times, then reached my cupped hand into the stream and dowsed the area for good measure. The searing pain persisted. I ignored it and waited.

After a few minutes, I struck the rock again, this time at the waterline. The spark extinguished with a tiny hiss and a puff of smoke. I put on my Polaroids and scanned the area. In the distance, I saw the rise of a fish, but it was not him. Could the pitch generated by the hammer not be right? I returned the hammer to the box, got up, and found a stone. I struck the rock and saw Moby immediately at the surface.

"I heard you the first time, Bob. I thought we decided that once was enough."

I paused to offer a reason, then decided to ignore

his comment. "I brought you something," I said as I reached into the box and retrieved a plastic container. I dumped four small fish into the water between Moby and me. He submerged, and each time he came up, he gulped one after the other until they were gone. Then he returned to face me.

"What were they?"

"Fresh sardines. They live in the ocean. Did you like them?"

"Did they taste good? Is that what you want to know?"

"No."

"Then what were you asking?"

"Were they good fish for you to eat?"

"Yes, they were. I feel more alive already."

"I must say, Moby, your speech seems clearer to me than before."

"Yes, removing the old hook made a big difference. I thank you again for that." I nodded. "There must be something else in that big box."

"Yes. I'd appreciate your help with something."

I removed from the box a strip of pine about three feet in length to which I had glued chunks of Styrofoam. I had painted the board in three colored segments—red, blue, and white. On each segment, I hammered in a tack not quite all the way, leaving a small gap under the head to which was tied about five feet of 6X tippet at the end of which were three midge pattern flies.

A hole was drilled in the center of this board through

which I tied thirty or so feet of clothesline cord.

His good eye was riveted on the device. "Are you asking if I think you can catch fish with that thing?"

I laughed. "No. It's not for that."

"Good. I didn't want to disappoint you."

Holding on to the end of the cord, I threw the contraption about twenty feet into a riffle, then carefully pulled it back in until it reached a spot where the current was slow and consistent. The flies slowly sorted themselves downstream until they were bobbing in place.

"Moby, kindly go downstream and turn around towards the flies. Let me know which one is most attractive to you."

He ducked under. I put on my sunglasses and could see his form make its way beyond the flies then approach them. He lingered a foot from them. I saw his head turn from side to side. Then he let himself drift a couple of feet downstream, where he returned to the flies for a second look. Then he went under them before surfacing in front of me.

"These are midges, right?"

"Yes," I said.

"The one associated with the white color was quite realistic. I believe a younger fish would go for it. The other two were no good."

"Why is that?"

"The movement of the legs was not natural. Too stiff."

"Thank you. This is very helpful. Would you mind

doing some more?"

"That would be fine."

I took out my index card, scribbled a note, and pulled the stick back in. In a few minutes, I had replaced the midges with three Blue Winged Olive patterns.

He was more charitable with these. I pulled in the stick. As I removed the flies, he said, "You know, Bob. There's more to it than picking the best fly."

"You mean presentation."

"Yes, that's very important. But there's something else."

"What else could there be?" I asked.

"I would call it *the wind*, but it's not like *your* wind. It's like the wind that moves under the water."

"You mean the current."

"No, it's nothing that you feel against your body. You feel it in a different way. It helps everything make sense, including what to eat." He ducked underwater, swam out, and returned. "The wind is everything in my world. I'm surprised it is not in yours." I could say nothing, and he could go no further with the explanation.

Like all animals, fish evolved over hundreds of millions of years. They have in their genes information that has helped them adapt to survive. Homo sapiens has been around half that time. Trout have thirty-eight to forty-two pairs of chromosomes to our paltry twenty-three. Why couldn't they have some special sensory abilities?

And so it went the next two visits. Sulfurs, tricos,

ants, beetles, hoppers. And Moby's choices all worked. He'd talk more about life underwater and the marvel of it all. In his way, he expressed how fortunate he felt to live another day when so many around him did not. And he would touch on the wind from time to time but always had to leave it hanging.

My world changed. Life slowed down. When I would be late for dinner, my wife would find me at my tying desk, staring at the wonder that is a feather. My time with family and friends took on new meaning—as did my time on the water, where I would spend more and more of it looking at the leaf and the leafhopper.

I looked forward to the time spent with this remarkable fish. I had come to consider him a special friend. Each visit went well beyond fishing advice. The leaning rock became my Delphi.

It was mid-November; Moby looked different.

"You've put on a little weight," I said. "The insects must have been plentiful."

"The midges, Blue Winged Olives, and tricos are the same. Beetles are much less."

"Isn't it spawning season for you?"

"Yes."

"But you have no kype?"

"Kype? Why would I have a kype?"

"Why wouldn't you?"

"I'm a female. Didn't you know?"

I nearly fell off the rock. "Oh my God!"

"I'll be leaving today to prepare my redd and lay my

eggs."

She looked at me, waiting for me to say something.

Finally, I said, "I guess we'll have to change your name from Moby P. to Moby V."

"Why? I'm happy with just Moby. I told you."

"Yes, we'll just stick with Moby."

"Yes, just Moby. She looked up at me. "Where's your color stick? Have you run out of flies?"

"I'll be using terrestrials for the next few months, and we've gone over those."

"Remember that with them presentation is important. They don't come up from the streambed; they come down from the sky. They drop *hard* onto the water. Their legs are stiff. They don't belong in the water and are not good swimmers."

As I nodded, I felt my eyes moisten.

"You humans. Always with the wet eyes. I'm glad we don't have to deal with that. Never let anything interfere with your vision, even for a moment, or you can be eaten."

"Good fish advice, as usual," was all I could muster.

"And Bob, think about the wind. I am sure you have something like that where you are. It's important to let it come into you, to be a part of you. We could all stand to be more content."

If there were ever a single word to describe her, it would be *content*.

"Will you return here after spawning?"

"Yes."

"Can we resume our talks?"

"Yes, of course," she said.

"Spending time with you has meant a lot to me."

"Me as well."

"Thank you… friend."

"Thank you, friend." And with that, she took a long look at me, ducked underwater, and began her way upstream.

As I was slowly leaving, I heard the tinkle of a fish breaking the water's surface. It was Moby.

"I have a confession," she said.

"Yes?"

"I let you catch me."

"No."

"Do you think I would have fallen for your ridiculous green fly?"

I laughed as I recalled the pathetic Woolly Bugger. "Why would you do that?"

"I was lonely."

"Why me? You could have taken the fly of any fisherman?"

"I watched you. I thought you might be lonely as well."

"I was. But why subject yourself to the pain of the hook and the pulling? Couldn't you just poke your head out of the water and talk to a fisherman?"

"I did do just that—twice."

"And?"

"Each time, there was a terrible sound, and they ran

off. The second man left his rod."

"Yes. I might have done the same."

"Well, I just wanted you to know."

"Thanks for that."

She let herself slowly sink, her good eye on me until the last possible moment; then, she turned and headed upstream.

I returned a month later, knocked on the rock, and waited for a long while before returning home.

When I came two weeks later, the stream was frozen over as far as I could see, and I left.

Two weeks after that, I returned. It had warmed to above freezing in the preceding days, and we had had more than average rainfall. The pull-off was puddled. I felt the pocket of my poncho for my pen and the index card full of new questions. I nearly slipped from the cool dark drizzle that coated everything. Morning now was only a slightly lighter version of night. I found a suitable stone and made my way to the leaning rock.

It was gone. In its place was a dripping ledge of mud. There were no other large rocks nearby. I put on my Polaroids. They only darkened the water. I laid my stone at the ledge, then added to it the ones from the pull-off. Then I added all I could find.

I became a much better fisherman, never as good as Tom or Brian, for sure, but very good.

I still don't know what Moby meant by *the wind*.

Someday I will. I'm sure of it.

Heather Visits Wallis
(Part 1 of 2)

"That's right, Heather, two hours," Heather's father said as he started to leave her room.

"Fuck! Two hours to make the most important decision of my life. Thanks a lot, Dad!"

"Don't get all dramatic on me, Heather. It's just your last two years of high school—and I'm paying for all four years of college."

"Do I have to pick my college now too?"

"No."

"Well. Thank God for small favors!"

"I don't have to do this, you know," he said.

"You're my fucking father. It's your job."

"And your mother's too. Why don't you ask her?"

She spun around toward the computer as the door slammed.

Staring for a moment at the blank screen, she Googled: Schools as far away as possible from fucking LA. There appeared page after page of sites showing schoolgirls wearing knee-high stockings, glasses, and school uniforms—all in sexually provocative poses. "Shit!" She entered *East Coast*, *High School*, *Boarding Schools*, *Peaceful*, *Rural*.

And that's how Heather Donlan transferred in her junior year of high school to the Oldfields School, the all-girls boarding school north of Baltimore.

Unlike her fellow students, many of whom had been there since the eighth grade, she knew no one. It didn't take long for word to get out about her recent life. Her parents had been in the middle of a nasty divorce when her mother arranged to have her father killed. The attempt failed; she, and her hitman lover, were jailed for life. Her father, who had been cheating on his wife for years, married his now-pregnant girlfriend and wanted nothing more to do with his former family—Heather and her older brother Sam.

Heather mostly just existed—a wallflower in life's dance. She was average, both in her studies and on the athletic field. Her brother, with whom she was never close, escaped into the Army as soon as he was of age and effectively disappeared from her life. If there was a fortunate side to any of this, it was that her father was well-off. Before flying the coop, he put money into a trust to pay for her education. With her mother off the grid, Heather was, for all practical purposes, an orphan in a strange new place.

Oldfields, founded in 1867, was on a beautiful campus in rural northern Baltimore County. It had horses and an abundance of open space. She liked horses but *loved* to run. Where she came from was the polar opposite—a McMansion in an exclusive development of a Los Angeles suburb.

Her dad made the call to the school. The application period had ended, but she had no doubt he'd get her in. He was always able to close the deal.

In no time, she was known to her fellow students as *the bitch*. Her teachers would describe her as bitter. She had been at the boarding school for only a week when her roommate, Kathy Brownlee, a transfer from a Minneapolis boarding school, requested a new roommate.

Heather attended her classes. Her teachers were kind and understanding. Today, more than any day, she needed to take a long run—not just around the campus with a couple of girls she didn't care to be with—she had done that every day since her arrival. What she needed was a long, cleansing run with trees and sunlight and country smells—alone.

She had heard about a running path near the school everyone called the NCR Trail. The official name was the Torrey C. Brown Trail. It was formerly the bed of the Northern Central Railroad that, since the 1800s, had carried passengers and freight between Baltimore and cities in Pennsylvania.

Students were not permitted off-campus without an adult. Miss Candace, Heather's math teacher, agreed to drive her to the trail at the end of class that day. Word went out, but no other students cared to go along—not surprising. So, right at 4:30 on a beautiful fall day, Heather hopped into Miss Candace's 2004 Subaru Forester and drove three-quarters of a mile down Glencoe Road to the small parking lot at the edge of the trail.

"I'll wait for you here," Miss Candace said.

"It's OK. I know the way back."

"I'm sure you do, hon, but those are the rules." She held up a stack of papers and said, "I have plenty of papers to grade. What better place to do it on such a gorgeous day? I've got a chair and a table in the back. I'll be just fine."

Heather nodded.

"I assume you'll be heading north from here," as she pointed in one direction. "I think it's prettier up that way."

Heather nodded again.

"Got your cell phone?"

Heather tapped her fanny pack, indicating it was there.

"Not that it makes much difference," Miss Candace said. "Reception is a bit spotty. How long will you be out for?"

"I could use an hour. Is that OK?"

"That's fine, hon. If you are later, try to call me. You have my number, right?

Heather nodded.

"Have a good run."

Heather did a few stretches, took a deep breath, then slowly began a jog. The dirt and dry leaves underfoot made a pleasant if unfamiliar sound. As she picked up speed, she became aware of the alive-dead smells of autumn on the East Coast, also new to her. She began to smile for the first time in months. The trees on the sides of the trail looked so different and so consumed her that she didn't see the signal until it loomed before her. She stopped in her tracks. *Jesus, I nearly ran into that thing. Looks like a giant lollipop.* Heather moved to the other side. At the top of the black metal pole, some twenty feet above her was a round, black metal clock-face at least five feet across. In place of hands were an odd arrangement of lights. There were seven altogether: three arranged vertically, with extra lights forming the upper right and lower left quadrants. The sign was just above eye level and explained that this thing was called "the 509 electrical light display block signal," and dated from the 1930s.

She looked at the arrangements of lights on the diagram then looked up at the big disc, trying to imagine how the lights might look to the engineer. Three vertical lights: "Clear Block. Proceed at normal speed." As she imagined the other two patterns, she heard a faint rumble followed by a shrill whistle coming from the south. The sounds grew louder. She felt a vibration through her running shoes, then heard a loud *ding ding ding* above her as she sensed a bright light. When she looked up at the signal, she saw the lights flashing randomly. Then she saw the smoke. It enveloped the entire trail from where she had just come. *Oh My God! Did something happen to Miss Candace? Did her car catch on fire? I've got to get back there.*

With her first step, the tip of her shoe caught, and she tumbled forward. She smelled oil. Her left hand rested on something hard and rough. She placed her right hand down to get to her feet and immediately gripped warm metal and saw her hand was resting on railroad track. *There weren't tracks here before.* She got to her feet. There was smoke everywhere. She moved to the side of the track and ran towards the smoke. She imagined seeing the car in flames. She wondered if she would be brave enough to rescue her teacher, or would she be too late and have to tell the headmistress that Miss Candace had died.

As she ran toward the smoke, a massive form emerged. Beside it, on the right, stood a small building Heather had not noticed before. *Wasn't that where Miss Candace had parked?* Neither Miss Candace nor her car was anywhere to be seen. Heather rubbed her eyes hard. When she looked ahead again, the form was unmistakable—the engine of a train, the kind she had only seen in the one cowboy movie her father ever took her to. As the smoke continued to clear, Heather saw that next to the house was a wagon with a pair of black horses. She walked towards the scene in a daze. People were going between the little house and the train. The women were dressed in long, dark dresses. Those who happened to glance her way quickly averted their eyes. It was now apparent to her that the house was a train station. The only thing that made sense to Heather was that she happened upon a film being shot. *But where did the tracks come from?* She hadn't seen them before. *And what about Miss Candace and her car? Had they been ushered off the set?*

A girl, Heather's age, appeared at the train car's

door. Like the other women, she was in a long, dark dress. *Yes. This is a film. Neat!* The Black man standing beside the carriage rushed over to the girl. She handed him a small cloth suitcase and a cardboard box. He took her hand and helped her down the steps. As he loaded her belongings into the carriage, she turned, her eyes meeting Heather's. The girl broke into a huge smile as she looked Heather up and down. She slowly walked toward Heather, stopping within six feet of her. She was Heather's height, thin, with striking cobalt eyes, and a strong, angular jaw.

"Don't you have any pride?" she asked.

"What the hell are you talking about?" Heather answered.

"Why, you're standing at a train station in your underwear."

"Underwear? This is my running clothing."

The girl walked around Heather.

"Are you crazy? Did you run away from the asylum?"

The carriage man walked up to the girl. "Miss Wallis. We should go."

The girl turned and said, "We'll go when I say we can go, Mr. Ned."

The girl extended her right hand. "Hi, I'm Wallis."

Heather cautiously shook hands. The girl's hand was soft, but her handshake was firm.

"Heather."

"So, Heather. Where are you running to—or from?"

"Nowhere. I'm just on a run."

Wallis' head went back as she laughed loudly. "You're just running? For no reason? And you're saying you're not crazy?"

"I'm not crazy, and I wish you'd stop fucking with me."

"Ha! You've got some spirit! And the language! What did you say your name was?"

"Heather."

"And my name's—"

"You told me your name already. Wallis. Isn't that a man's name?"

"Mine is spelled W-A-L-L-I-S. Not like the man's name. I'm probably the only woman with that name!"

"Nope."

"What? You know another female Wallis?"

"There was a Wallis Simpson who became famous."

"Famous? For what?"

Heather shrugged. "I just read it somewhere. She could have been a murderer for all I know. Hey, maybe that *was* you."

The coachman stepped forward and, in a loud whisper, said, "This young lady is clearly not right, Miss Wallis. I don't think you should be speaking to her."

"I'll speak to whomever I please, and she herself told me she's not crazy. Isn't that right, Heather?"

Heather nodded, then nervously said, "See you never," and started to back away.

"Where are you going?" asked Wallis.

"I want to check on Miss Candace from the school."

"School. There's only one school around here, and it's the one I go to. Which school do you go to?"

"Oldfields."

"Oldfields? Maybe you are crazy after all."

"Why do you keep saying such stupid things?"

"There are fifty-nine students at Oldfields, and I know every one of them. And I certainly would remember a student who runs for no reason and in her underwear, no less."

Wallis looked up at the sky, then back at Heather. "OK then. Tell me this. Are you Courtesy or Gentleness?"

"What the hell are you talking about?"

"You said you were at my school. All the students are divided into two teams—Courtesy and Gentleness. You have to be one or the other. So, are you Courtesy or Gentleness?"

"Well, I don't know which Oldfields you go to, but my Oldfields in 2020 divides us into White or Green teams. I'm White."

"Wait. What did you say about 2020?"

"The year 2020."

"What are you talking about? This is 1913."

"You mean in the movie."

"Movie? What movie?"

"This movie! All this is a movie," Heather said emphatically, spreading her arms.

"I can assure you this is no movie."

"It's not?"

Wallis shook her head. "Where do you live on

campus?"

"Centennial Dorm."

"There's no Centennial Dorm."

"Of course there is. It's my dorm."

"Where is it, then?

"It's attached to Old House."

Wallis turned to Mr. Ned, who shrugged, then back at Heather, and said quietly, "There is Old House. That's the main building."

"I've got to find Miss Candace," Heather said, backing away again.

Wallis scanned the area. "I'd say Miss Candace has gone, Heather. You'll come back with us."

"No way in hell I'm doing that!"

Before Heather could get out of range, Wallis grabbed her elbow and ushered her to the coach.

"You'll sit in the back next to me."

Once the two of them were seated, Wallis said, "Mr. Ned?"

"Yes, ma'am."

"Now listen to me. I want you to drive back as slow as you can without looking suspicious. You understand?"

"Yes, ma'am."

"And don't you dare look back here until we get to the school. You understand?"

"But Miss Wallis. You know how strict Miss Nan is. If we're late, we're in big trouble."

"Let me worry about Miss Nan. One more thing. From now on, this girl isn't Heather. She's my cousin

Louise from Richmond, and she came with me on the train."

"But you know the rules, Miss Wallis."

"I know all about the rules, Mr. Ned," and whispered to Heather, "and how to get around them. Now help me out of my dress."

"What? I'm outta here," shouted Heather.

Heather got one leg out of the coach when Wallis pulled her back in.

"You think I could get you into the school looking like that? You're putting this dress on over your *running* clothing."

"What will you wear?"

"My new dress—from the best shop in Baltimore." Wallis pointed to the box next to her. "Now, don't dilly-dally."

The rear of the coach became a flutter of cloth and shrieks. The switch was completed as a grinning Mr. Ned eased his carriage up to Old House.

He hopped out and opened the door. "Here you are, ladies. Miss Wallis," and here he said a little louder, "Miss Louise."

"Miss Wallis. Do you need help with your things?"

"Louise and I can handle them. Don't you forget this is secret."

"Don't worry about me, Miss Wallis."

As Wallis unloaded her things, she saw Heather staring at Old House.

Wallis asked, "Does it look familiar?"

"Kind of. What there is of it."

"Where's your dorm?

"Not here." Heather shielded her eyes and scanned the immediate area. "Neither is anything else."

"What else are you referring to, sweetie?"

Heather pointing from left to right, "That's where The Commons would be. Then The Garden House. Then the Headmaster's house. Then Carroll House."

Heather was still staring into the fields and trees when Wallis said, "Never mind all that. Let's go in. I can't wait for you to meet Mary, my roommate."

Heather grabbed the box and opened the door for Wallis. As they crossed the parlor, Heather suddenly stopped.

"Why did you stop?"

Heather pointed her head towards an older woman standing at the other end of the room, staring at her. "Who's that woman?" she whispered.

"That's Miss Nan, the principal."

"She's freaks me out," said Heather.

"Freaks you out? What in heaven's name does that mean?"

"Spooky. She's spooky."

Wallis glanced towards the woman and shrugged. "That's the way she always looks. And she happens to be very nice on the inside."

Heather murmured, "Yeah, deep inside."

"Let's get going."

Wallis opened the door to the stairs. They made their

way up the three flights of creaky, wooden steps. Wallis pushed her way through the door and led Heather down the hall.

"Welcome to Heaven," Wallis said.

"Heaven? I didn't know we were dead."

Wallis stopped, turned around to face Heather, and laughed. Then Heather laughed.

"We call the top floor Heaven," Wallis said.

Wallis led Heather to a door and knocked while saying, "Knock knock."

The door was opened by Mary Kirk, a petite young woman in a sailor dress.

"It's about time you got here. Did you get lost in Baltimore?"

"I can't get here any sooner than the train brings me here, Mary," Wallis said. She then stepped to the side. "I'd like you to meet my cousin Heather—I mean Louise."

Mary squinted. Heather and Wallis looked uncomfortably at each other.

"Lordy! Looks like you are losing your touch, Wallis."

Mary turned to Heather and said, "Who are you really?"

Wallis sighed and ushered Heather into the room.

"This is Heather," Wallis said.

"Are you certain?"

Wallis and Heather nodded.

"And why are you wearing Wallis' dress?

"Take the dress off, Heather," Wallis said.

Heather struggled to get the dress off over her head. She stood there in her running clothing.

"This is how I found her at the train station," Wallis said.

"My running clothes."

"Running clothes?" Mary blurted. "What on earth?"

"Heather likes to run," Wallis said.

"Yeah, I do."

"Heather thought I was in a movie. Isn't that right, Heather?"

Heather nodded.

"You? A movie star?" Mary said to Wallis.

"I *could too* be a movie star," insisted Wallis.

"Who would want someone as skinny as you in their movie?" Mary chuckled.

"See. It's fine to laugh, Heather. Mary, you know Heather said something quite funny as we arrived."

"Really? What did she say?"

"I told her this floor is called Heaven, and she said 'Heaven? I didn't know we were dead?'"

Wallis and Mary laughed. "I thought *we* were rather gay," said Wallis, "but you certainly can be as well."

"I'm not gay!"

"OK, dear," said Wallis. "I was just giving you a compliment. Mary, make a note for the record that Heather is not gay."

Mary pretended to be writing in a book, as she said, "Heather—not gay."

"Heather is from the future, Mary. 2020. Isn't that

right, Heather?"

Heather nodded.

Mary and Wallis looked at each other and started to laugh.

"Why are you laughing? It's true."

They laughed again.

"And to top it off, she's a student at Oldfields," Wallis added. "Centennial Dorm. Isn't that right, Heather?"

"Yeah."

"Centennial? Where's that?" asked Mary, holding back a laugh.

Heather stepped toward Wallis and shoved her, forcing her to stumble back several steps. "Why did you bring me here? To make fun of me? To show me off to your little friends, bitch!"

Wallis smiled and said, "Wow! What language! Maybe... but I'm not all bad, am I Mary? I couldn't just leave you at the station waiting for your imaginary Miss Candace."

"Who's Miss Candace?" Mary asked.

"My math teacher. And she's real."

"What classes are you taking then?" Mary asked.

"English, U.S. History, Chemistry, Algebra II, and Spanish."

Wallis and Mary looked at each other, then at Heather.

"You seem so serious, Heather," said Mary.

"I'd say angry," added Wallis.

Wallis turned to Heather. "Heather dear. Mary and

I are just concerned about you. Girls need to be gay. I would venture to say that of all the girls here at Oldfields, we are the gayest."

"Why do you keep bringing up this *gay* stuff?"

"Because, Heather, if you're not gay, you'll never get a beau," said Mary. "You only have one chance to make a first impression."

"Yeah. I've heard that," Heather muttered.

"Quite important when it comes to hooking a beau. Isn't that right, Wallis?" Mary said.

"Words I live by. The boys prefer girls who are gay."

"What?"

"Do you have a beau, Heather?" Mary asked.

"What's that?"

"If she doesn't know what that is, I think it's safe to say she doesn't have one," Wallis laughed.

"Just tell me what it means."

"A boyfriend," said Mary.

"You mean a girlfriend," Heather said.

Mary and Wallis stared at her.

"Since I got here, it's been that you're *gay* and that I have to be *gay*." Heather frowned, then blurted, "Listen. I don't know who the hell you are or what the hell is going on around here. I go out for a run to clear my head and get kidnapped by a nutcase who says she's from 1913 and forces me into a carriage and makes me put on this old-fashioned dress."

"Old fashioned? I'll have you know it's the very height of fashion."

"Right! Something my fucking grandma wouldn't even wear!"

"Good Lord! Do you hear her, Mary? And I thought I had the habit of speaking my mind."

"I'll have you know we're very fashionable," Mary added.

"You? Fashionable? With you being so *gay* and in that sailor get-up, I would take you for an admiral in the lesbian navy."

"Well, I never!" Mary exclaimed.

Wallis broke into laughter. "Heather, what do you think *gay* means?"

"You think I'm stupid?" said Heather.

"No. We don't think you're stupid," said Wallis. "What is the definition of *gay*?"

"Homosexual."

Mary broke out laughing.

"Homosexual? Where on earth did you get that from?" asked Mary.

"Everybody knows that."

"Everybody in 2020?" asked Mary.

"That's right. Everybody in 2020. So, what does *gay* mean to you?"

"Lighthearted," said Wallis. "A fellow wants a girl who's lighthearted—not some old sourpuss. Are you a sourpuss, Heather?"

"OK. I'm not lighthearted, but I've had a lot of shit to deal with."

"Shit?" asked Wallis.

"Yeah. Shit," said Heather.

Wallis and Mary looked at each other and shrugged.

"It seems like everybody's got problems, Heather. What are yours?" Mary asked.

"My mom's in prison—for life—and Dad's disappeared with his new girlfriend. My brother's in the army and never speaks to me. And I don't have any friends. Is that enough for you?"

"Oh my! That is terrible," Mary said. "Well, Wallis' father died when she was a baby, and if her mother didn't remarry that dreadfully boring man, she'd still be living in that crummy apartment in Baltimore. And she has to beg her uncle for money."

"You just have to take the cards you're dealt and make the best of them," said Wallis. "We all have... *shit*... in our lives. And you have to learn to be the hammer, not the nail—even if you're a woman... I'd bet you've been the nail."

Heather nodded and started to cry. Wallis and Mary hugged her. Then Wallis looked at Heather and said, "But Heather, dear, regarding the hammer, it must not be the big heavy kind a roustabout would use putting up the circus tent. It must be the small kind that goes *tap tap tap* and gradually gets you what you want."

"Like the way a silversmith makes a pattern in a chafing dish," added Mary.

"And Mary knows about silver. Her family is in the business."

"Do you believe in signs, Heather?" Mary asked.

"Do I believe in signs? What the hell are you talking about?"

"Let me give you an example," said Mary. "Wallis and I are the best of friends, right?"

"If you say so."

"My name begins with an *M*, and Wallis's begins with a *W*. If I turn my *M* upside down, what do you have?"

Heather stared at Mary in disbelief. "Are you fucking kidding me?"

"Why no, I'm not kidding you. Don't you get it? An *M* becomes a *W*. Isn't that special?"

"And if I turn my *H* upside down, what do I have, Mary?

Mary nervously looked over to Wallis, who was grinning and said, "You still have an *H*, I guess."

"Isn't that fucking special! Why I'll bet my *H* is more special than either of your letters." Wallis broke out into laughter. "Damn. If this is an example of the higher education you get at Oldfields, I made the wrong decision!" Heather added.

Wallis put her arm around Heather's shoulders and said, "As long as you're here, you've got us as friends. Right, Mary?"

"… Yes. OK. And we're the most popular girls in the school if I do say so myself."

"You have said that," said Heather. "And what about you, Mary? What's wrong with your life?"

"You. You're what's wrong."

"Me? Why am I your problem?"

"Because you make me so sad." Mary stepped close to Heather and said, "And I would feel better if I knew you weren't crazy. How do we know you're really from 2020? You can't prove it, can you."

"I can too!"

"Who's the president, then?" asked Mary.

"Donald Trump."

"Trump? What kind of name is that?" asked Wallis.

"What the hell kind of name is Wallis?" replied Heather.

"Touché!" said Wallis. "Since we're not from the future, we can't disprove that. Can we, Mary?"

"The fact is we can't disprove anything you *tell* us," said Mary. "Show us something."

Heather felt her shorts for a pocket. There was none. Then she saw her fanny pack and unzipped it, pulling out her cell phone.

"My cell phone."

"Cell phone? What's that?" asked Wallis.

"A telephone."

"That little thing!" said Mary.

"Show us how it works," said Wallis.

Heather pulled the phone back toward her. "No."

"No? Why not?" asked Mary.

"Not until I hear both of you curse."

"Never. I don't care if I ever see your phone thing," said Mary.

"And why not?" asked Heather.

"Because it's vulgar and unladylike. Isn't that right, Wallis?"

"That's right. It's unbecoming of young women."

"So, Mary, you're dressed like a sailor. You mean to say you can't act like a sailor for one second and give me one curse word?" Heather asked as she brought the cell phone close to Mary's eyes then drew it back.

Mary hesitated and said, "No. No, I can't."

"Fuck! There! I said it," said Wallis.

"Wallis!" blurted Mary.

"How did it feel?" asked Heather.

Wallis nodded. "I must admit, it felt good. Now show me the phone."

"Sorry, you both must do it."

"All right, I'll say it one time very softly," said Mary.

"Oh, it's too late for that. You missed your chance," Heather said as she put her cell back in her fanny pack.

"What must I do then?"

"I'll bet you're good at grammar," Heather said.

Mary nodded.

"Good. I'm going to give you a chance to show off your Oldfields education."

Mary frowned, and her eyes began to water.

Heather held Mary's shoulders and looked her in the eyes. "Oh, don't cry. You must always be gay," said Heather. "Remember the curse word Wallis said?" Mary nodded. "Conjugate it."

Mary just stared. Heather raised her eyebrows to tell her to get on with it.

"I… Which tense?"

"Your choice," said Heather.

"All right… Present."

"Good enough," said Heather.

Mary started to cry.

"Come on, Mary. Just get it over with," begged Wallis.

"You both swear on your mothers' graves you won't breathe a word of this?" said Mary.

"Our mothers are still alive. You must pick something else," said Wallis.

"All right then. Do you swear on our friendship that you won't breathe a word of this to anyone?"

"I do," said Wallis and Heather at the same time, then giggled.

"Could I possibly do a different word, Heather? That one is so bad."

"Why do you think she picked it?" Wallis said.

"Yes. *Fuck* is the queen of curse words," said Heather. Then she and Wallis flashed each other the same wicked smile.

Mary motioned them to gather close. She brought their shoulders down into a tight huddle, then whispered at breakneck speed, "I fuck, you fuck, he/she/it fucks, we fuck, you fuck, they fuck."

Mary's face went from mortification to grinning as they all laughed and hugged.

Heather triumphantly retrieved the cell phone from her pack and showed it to the girls.

"You press these numbers to make the call."

"For Lord's sake, call someone," said Mary.

"I don't have anyone to call… I know. I'll call the school. I have the number in my phone book… Here it is." Heather pressed ten numbers. Each time there was a beep that delighted the girls. Then silence. Heather looked at the phone. "I can't make a call. There's no signal."

Wallis put her arm on Heather's shoulder. "Think, Heather. Isn't there anything else that little contraption can do to knock us dead?"

A smile crept onto Heather's lips. "Yeah. I have a game on here." She flicked through groups of tiny icons as the girls stared in amazement. "Here it is!"

"What is it?" asked Mary.

"Subway Surfer."

"Subway… what?" asked Wallis.

"Surfer. Never mind. Anyway, this guy is tagging the train."

"Tagging? What's that?" asked Mary.

"Spray-painting his initials."

"What's spray-painting?" asked Wallis.

"Do I have to explain every freaking thing to you? It's paint that sprays out of a can. I guess you don't have that, do you?"

"No. We don't," said Wallis.

"But we do have… uh… escalators," Mary said.

"And… umm… vacuum cleaners," said Wallis.

Heather shook her head. "Good for you. Now watch

this." She held out the phone. Both girls huddled close; Heather tapped the screen. "The boy in the hoodie is tagging the train."

"Oh no. The policeman is after him," said Mary.

"He's running down the track. Oh no. There's a barrier," said Wallis.

Heather deftly flicked her finger, and the boy jumped the barrier, then she swiped to steer him left and right to other tracks and avoid more obstacles, the policeman in hot pursuit. "Now watch this." Heather swiped down, and the boy slid under a barrier and kept running. The girls giggled and screamed.

"You're controlling the boy?" Wallis marveled.

"Yep."

"The cop is still after him," Mary said.

A high wall loomed ahead. Both girls gasped, eyes gaping. Heather tapped the screen; a hoverboard materialized under the boy, and he sailed over the wall. Heather kept the boy running as lights blinked and sounds never heard by the girls spouted from the phone. The boy finally collided with a train car and was nabbed by the cop.

"Oh no. What's going to happen to him?" asked Mary.

"Will he go to jail?" asked Wallis.

Heather shook her head.

"No. You just start it up again. IT'S A GAME, LADIES!"

"May I try it?" asked Wallis.

Wallis giggled as Heather turned over the phone and explained how to work the game.

"I gotta pee. Where's the bathroom?" asked Heather.

"Off the parlor on the first floor," said Mary.

Heather began to leave when Wallis said, "Stop. You can't go out like that. Put my dress back on."

Heather put on the dress as the girls immersed themselves in Subway Surfer. She found the bathroom and was thankful Miss Nan was nowhere to be seen. Marveling at the water closet toilet, Heather figured out that you have to pull the chain to make it flush. When she exited, Miss Nan stood before her, holding out a ticket.

"Your ticket," said Miss Nan.

"A ticket for the bathroom?"

Miss Nan broke out into a huge smile. "No, dear. Your train. Here, take it." She reached into the pocket of her dress and pulled out a pocket watch, pressed a button, and the cover popped open. "It leaves in nine minutes."

Then she reached into her other pocket and pulled out a small bag. "And a little snack for the trip."

Heather peeked inside the bag. "An orange. I love oranges."

"I know."

"But what about my friends?"

"Wallis and Mary will be fine." Miss Nan smiled, then asked, "Tell me, dear, do you peel your oranges or just bite into them?"

"I peel them, of course."

"Why not just eat them like an apple?"

"Because the peel is bitter. If you just bite into it, it will ruin the whole thing."

"That's right, dear. Just so you understand."

Then Miss Nan reached up and grasped Heather's head with both hands. Heather was still for a moment, then jumped back.

"Ow! What the hell was that?"

"Sorry, dear. It must have been static electricity."

"Jesus!" said Heather as she backed away.

"Don't dilly-dally. It's the last train."

Heather gave a nervous smile before hurrying out of the building. *Crazy lady. Can't wait to get the hell out of here!*

Once on Glencoe Road, Heather hiked up her dress and ran. Moments later, she saw the cloud of steam coming from the train and heard the "All aboard." She hopped up the steps and saw she was the only passenger in the car. The conductor's voice grew louder. "All aboard. Train to Baltimore. All aboard." The conductor entered the passenger car. He was a friendly-looking, bespectacled middle-aged man with a mustache. "Tickets. Tickets, please."

He stood before Heather. "Where to, Miss?"

"Umm…"

"Just look at your ticket," he said.

"Glencoe? But *this* is Glencoe."

The conductor took her ticket and smiled warmly, "Have a pleasant ride, Miss." There was another loud "All aboard," and he was gone.

She looked through the window and saw the trees at the height of their fall brilliance. Pushing the window open, she inhaled the smell of autumn and smiled.

So much has happened. I have new friends. They like me. But where am I? And where am I going? Will I ever get home? Will I ever see Wallis and Mary again? What about Miss Candace? Is she OK?

She peeled the orange and savored its sweetness. As she put the peels into the bag, she heard the distant *ding ding ding* of the signal. The cabin suddenly became a ball of bright white light. Heather's hands flew up to her face to cover her eyes. Her breath caught as she felt herself fall like riding the downward track of a roller coaster. Her back and head hit the ground hard.

She opened her eyes, took a deep breath, and again smelled the autumn woods. As the heavy mist cleared, she found herself alone on the trail. She got to her feet. The dress was dusty and caked with dirt; she took it off and rolled it tightly. Miss Candace was asleep in her chair.

A breeze carried off the paper bag before she could catch it. She kneeled to pick up the peels. A strong gust of wind picked them up and scattered them down the trail, out of sight.

As she got to her feet, tears were welling in her eyes.

She cried. It was a cry that came from all the times in her life she should have cried.

Miss Candace rushed over and held her for a long, long time.

Wallis Visits Heather (Part 2 of 2)

At precisely 4:45 PM, there was a knock at Miss Nan's door.

"Come in, Wallis."

Wallis entered and closed the door behind her. "Thank you for seeing me, Miss Nan."

"What's the urgency?"

"My friend Heather—"

"Ah yes. Your friend from… elsewhere," said Miss Nan.

"You helped her with that train home."

"And you will recall you and Mary swore an oath to me that you would not breathe a word of this to anyone."

"And we haven't, Miss Nan. I swear to God we haven't."

"OK. I believe you. How can I help you?"

"You see… she has my dress… "

"I recall seeing the young lady wearing a dress that could have been yours, yes."

"And I would like to see her and get it back."

"You mean to tell me that you would risk your life over an ordinary dress? Have you lost your mind, Wallis Warfield?"

"I also have this." Wallis held up Heather's cell phone. Miss Nan paused then extended her hand.

"May I see it?"

"Yes, ma'am." Wallis handed it to her.

"What is it?

"A telephone from her time. You can also play the most wonderful games on it."

"And you want to return this telephone device to her."

"Yes, ma'am."

"Show me how it works."

"It stopped working after a few hours."

"So, it's broken."

"I don't know."

"And I'll repeat it. You're willing to risk your life for a dress and a broken thing?"

"You did it for Heather. Weren't you risking her life?"

"Yes. But Heather came into our world by accident and had no place here. There was a window during which it was possible."

"So you believe it was an accident she came here?"

"You don't?"

"No, ma'am. I think there was a reason she came."

"All right. I'll grant you that's possible," said Miss Nan.

"And this window you spoke of has closed?"

"No, but it may be closing." Miss Nan looked at Wallis with both sternness and love.

"It's not really about the dress or the phone, Miss

Nan. It's more important than that."

"I should hope so. What is it, then?"

"My destiny."

"Your destiny."

"Heather said she had heard of another woman named Wallis Simpson who was famous. This woman spelled her first name like I do."

"What was she famous for?"

"She couldn't say."

"And you think that was you?"

"Yes. I've thought of nothing else since Heather left."

"Wallis, you'll be the death of me. You think you're quite the woman of the world, but in truth, you're a seventeen-year-old girl who has never left Baltimore. You are my responsibility, you know. What would I say to your mother and step-father if you didn't come back?"

Wallis closed her eyes and put her head down in thought. After a few moments, her head raised, her eyes opened, and she looked into Miss Nan's eyes.

"I shall write a letter in which I will state that I feel my life is hopeless, and I no longer want to be a burden on my family. That I have decided to leave Oldfields and end my life in a way that will not disgrace my school or family. You will say you found this letter under your door just before I disappeared."

"And Mary?"

"Mary can keep a secret."

"And if I say no?"

"What could I do? You hold all the cards."

"Come back in twenty minutes."

"Yes, ma'am."

Wallis started to leave.

"Wallis."

Wallis turned around.

"Bring the letter. Slide it under my door, then knock."

Miss Nan locked her door. She pushed a stepstool over to the tall bookcase and, standing on tiptoe, removed a worn leather-bound volume from the top shelf. Returning to her desk, Miss Nan opened the book and withdrew a folded paper from a slit under a bookplate inside the front cover. She opened her pocket watch and placed it on the desk. Then, taking her magnifying glass, studied page after page of the book, then the document, back and forth, all the while glancing at the watch. She removed a slide-rule and a slip of paper from the top drawer and, using the slide-rule with great speed, jotted down her calculations. She drew open the curtains and the window and spent a few moments gazing at the late afternoon sky.

Then she unlocked the bottom drawer of her desk, removed a metal box, and placed it on the desk. She opened it with the smallest key on her massive key ring. She removed two tickets and another smaller box from this box, placing them on the desk. This diminutive wooden cube, bound with iron bands, measured no more than four inches on each side. She removed her spectacles and put on a pair with dark lenses. She unlocked this small box. As she raised the lid, a pulsating purple light filled the room. Miss Nan lowered her head over the open box, holding her hands like blinders to the sides of her face to concentrate the light into her eyes. She took several deep breaths as she murmured into the box, then carried it to the window and held it up; then she returned everything to its place within her desk except for the tickets.

She referred to the slip of paper once more, nodded, sighed, and wrote on the tickets. Lighting a match, she burned the paper with the calculations.

Right on time, Miss Nan heard the hiss of the envelope sliding onto her office floor, followed by a knock. She kicked the letter to the side, let Wallis in, locked the door behind her, and handed Wallis the two tickets.

"Look at these carefully, Wallis."

"I leave tomorrow morning at 7:40."

"No! No! No! The *train* leaves at 7:40. You must be at the Glencoe Station no later than 7:35. The train will leave promptly. You will be the only passenger. You will give the conductor your ticket. He will know what to do."

"Yes, ma'am."

"When you arrive, take stock of exactly where you are. Memorize the trees and the rocks. That's where the train will pick you up for your return, so be sure to place yourself safely to the side of the tracks."

"Yes, ma'am."

"The other ticket is for the return. Guard it with

your life because your life truly depends upon it. You will have only a short time with Heather."

Wallis nodded. "Miss Nan, what would happen if I decided to stay longer with my friend?"

"IF *YOU* DECIDED? Perish the thought, young lady! Understand that time is a tricky thing, and this type of travel carries a great deal of risk. Accidents can happen. How do you think Heather ended up here? She just happened to be at the signal at the wrong time. I felt an obligation to try to make things right for her, the poor thing."

"Yes, ma'am."

"Do you remember Sadie Bremer from last year's graduating class?"

"Yes. She was the one who drowned, and they never found her body."

"She didn't drown."

Wallis gasped and looked down at the two tickets.

"Do you have any questions, dear?"

"No, ma'am."

"Take my hand."

Miss Nan led Wallis to a crucifix on the wall. "Lord Jesus, I beseech you to protect this child on her journey. May it be all she needs it to be. And may she return to the bosom of her family and her school safe and sound." Wallis joined her in the *Amen*.

Miss Nan embraced Wallis. "Can you keep another secret, Wallis?"

"Yes, ma'am."

"You've always been one of my favorites."

"Thank you, Miss Nan. How can I ever repay you?"

"Never ever ask to do this again! You know I won't sleep until you return. And if something happened to you, I don't know what I would do. But if you become famous or rich, I'd like you to remember this school and be generous. Oldfields is my life and will have been yours for a time. That's how I'd like to be repaid." Wallis nodded. "Get plenty of rest. You'll need a clear head. I'll tap on your door at six-thirty."

Wallis started out the door when she heard Miss Nan call her name.

A smiling Miss Nan said, "I hope you're not famous for a bad reason."

Wallis laughed and whispered, "You know when Heather was so cross with me, she said maybe I'll turn out to be a famous murderer."

"God forbid!"

Wallis didn't sleep that night. She was wide awake to hear the soft knock. She quietly left Old House as the first hint of sunrise lightened the morning sky.

***

Heather awoke to her name being called in a loud whisper from the other side of the door. She lumbered over in her pajamas.

"Who is it?"

"Wallis. Let me in before someone sees me."

The voice sounded familiar. Heather woke up fully

and shouted: "Wallis!" She flung the door open to see her friend. Grabbing Wallis' arm, she jerked her inside and locked the door. They embraced and laughed.

"I thought I'd never see you again," said Heather.

"You either," Wallis said, laughing.

"Let me look at you." Heather took a step back, took one look at Wallis, and began laughing. "What the hell are you doing in your underwear?"

"I saw the way you were dressed and thought I'd better look the same so as not to raise attention. The best I could do was to cut off the ends of my bloomers and the sleeves from my blouse to make my running costume."

"But your shoes? I don't think lace-up leather high-top shoes would qualify as running shoes."

"They're all I had!"

Heather hugged her again. "I'll take you any way, Wallis, stupid-ass outfit and all."

Wallis looked around the room. "Where's your roommate?"

"She split a few days ago."

"Split? Oh my God. That's horrible!"

"It was OK."

"How could it be OK with all her insides coming out!"

Heather exploded with laughter. "*Split* means she left."

Wallis held out the phone.

"My phone!"

"It stopped working."

"Just needs more juice."

"Juice?" asked Wallis.

"Electricity. I just need to attach it to this cable." Heather plugged in her phone, then went to the drawer and pulled out Wallis' dress. "I believe this is yours, ma'am."

"I believe it is. I'm surprised you're not wearing it around here."

"Yeah, right. Here, sit next to me." Heather motioned for her to sit on the bed. "I had a dream about you last night."

"Really?"

"You were lost in a forest and calling out for anyone to help you. It was getting dark, and your cries became more desperate."

"Did I make it out safely?"

"Yes. I showed up from out of nowhere with a compass and a map. The funny thing is I don't know how to use a compass or read a map."

"Thank you."

"It was just a dream."

"I know."

Wallis looked at Heather. "I think you've changed, Heather. Are you happier?"

"Yes, I am. In fact, you could say I'm quite *gay*."

They both laughed.

"Why did you come, Wallis? I know there must be a better reason than just to return my phone and get your dress back."

"Do you remember telling me that you had heard of a Wallis Simpson?"

"Yes."

"And that this person was famous."

"Yes. And that was all I really knew... then."

"Am I that person?"

"Yes."

"I didn't become a murderer, did I?"

"No, you didn't... Wallis. Wait a second. Let me see your ticket home."

Wallis showed her the ticket.

"You leave this evening on the 8:10 train. It'll be dark by then. That's good, but that doesn't give us much time to be together. You might want to see how things have changed at Oldfields. It's good you came on a Saturday. I'm free all day."

"Perhaps, later. Heather, I must learn what I will become. How many people have that opportunity?"

"None. But how many really want to know?"

"Wouldn't you?"

"No."

"Why not?"

"Life wouldn't be the same if I knew what was down the road. It wouldn't be an adventure. I'm kind of surprised you don't think that way too."

"When you said I would be famous, I just couldn't leave it at that. I have to know. Do you know what became of me?"

"Yes. I read everything about your life I could get my

hands on. You are undoubtedly the most famous person ever to graduate from Oldfields."

"Was I known outside the area?"

"You were known throughout the world."

"Throughout the world! You must show me the book."

"Book? There are *books*, Wallis. And articles."

"If we are really good friends, you'll show me everything!"

"It's because we are good friends that I am asking you to reconsider."

"But I came—" Heather held her hand up, and Wallis stopped.

"OK. Ask me a question. Maybe I'll answer it," said Heather.

"This is torture! You're not my friend! Mary would never do this to me."

"I'm not Mary. Ask me a question, Wallis."

Wallis pouted, turned her head away, then turned to Heather. "Did I marry?"

"Yes."

"Once?"

Heather held up three fingers.

"Three times! My God! I presume Mr. Simpson was the third."

Heather shook her head. "The second."

"Was I happy?"

"At times."

"You're being most unhelpful!"

"Wallis, what will you do with the information? How would knowing what you became help you now?"

"Maybe I could change certain things and make a difference."

"A difference to you, or your family, or the world?"

"All three, I guess."

"You guess! You really haven't thought this through, have you? Who's to say one is even able to change the future. Did you discuss this with Miss Nan?"

"Not in depth."

"So, what is the real reason you came?"

"It's all your fault, Heather!"

"My fault?"

"For telling me I might be this Wallis Simpson—who became famous."

"All right. I will own up to my part in this. So the truth is that you simply can't stand not to know. Is that right?"

"Yes! I've hardly slept since you left. I want to finally put to rest these thoughts swimming around in my head."

Heather walked over to her closet, pulled out some jeans and sandals, and took a top from her dresser. Heather looked her over. "Here, put these on. And that hairstyle!" She shook her head and handed Wallis an Orioles baseball cap.

"We're going to take a little walk to Miss Nan's," said Heather.

"She can't still be alive!"

"No, the room named after her."

On the way to Old House from the dorm, Wallis was amazed at how the campus had changed and was relieved to get back to the one building she knew. *Miss Nan's* had been the library in her day. The beautiful room was tastefully decorated. There were comfortable chairs and couches within the perimeter of bookcases and paintings. Wallis was drawn immediately to the portrait of Miss Nan at the far end of the room. It showed the principal serenely knitting. Wallis stood in front of the painting for quite some time before her gaze went down to the inscription:

ANNA GREEN MCCULLOUGH
1848 -1928
PRINCIPAL 1904 -1928.

She turned to Heather, blotting her tears, "She died in 1928. She was still principal when she died. She was—I mean, *is*—a great woman."

Heather led Wallis to a small table on the side of the room. On the table were four objects: a photo of Wallis as a young woman, a photo of The Duke and Duchess of Windsor, a brief bio of Wallis' time at Oldfields, and a three-volume Sotheby's 1997 auction catalog of the Duke and Duchess's possessions. While she was looking at her photo, a student walked by and said, "You know, you look like her."

"She hears that a lot," said Heather. The girl smiled and walked off.

"This is me?" Wallis asked, in a way that made Heather feel her friend didn't want it to be true. "I became British Royalty?"

"Yes, but it's more complicated than that."

"And the Duke of Windsor was my third husband?"

"Yes."

"When did we marry?"

"1937."

Wallis picked up the picture of a smiling Duke and Duchess.

"This is us?"

"Yes."

"We look happy."

"The picture shows a happy time."

She thumbed through the three-volume auction catalog. Heather looked for a reaction but saw only a tight smile.

"I can't believe we had all these beautiful things," said Wallis in a monotone.

Then she read the framed one-page bio that spoke of Wallis' time at Oldfields. It described her as "a popular girl with a strong sense of camaraderie." It went on to a quote describing her close relationship with Miss Nan. "She took me for walks along the paths behind the school. She talked to me quietly about my studies, Christian inspiration, the mixed joys and sadness of youth. The ache gradually went away."

On reading this, Wallis whispered, "How true," and looked over her shoulder at the portrait of Miss Nan.

She breathed heavily as she read the last paragraph: "Wallis Warfield Simpson made a lasting impression in history when she married the Duke of Windsor on June 3, 1937. Edward VIII had abdicated the English throne in late 1936 to be free to marry her. Their marriage ended with his death in 1972. The Duchess of Windsor died in Paris in 1986."

"I died in 1986... In Paris... Does *abdicated the English throne* mean what I think it does?" asked Wallis as she turned slightly towards Heather.

"It means that he was next in line to be King of England and gave it up to marry the woman he loved."

"Me."

"Yes."

"I see."

"This doesn't make you happy, does it, Wallis?"

"No... I don't know why. I think it would have made me positively giddy had you told me this on your visit. My God! To be the Duchess of Windsor! Why am I not happy, Heather?"

At that moment, another student came by and said, "Interesting, isn't it? It's amazing to think that she was a student here just like us." Wallis nodded without looking at the girl. "You know, if you want to learn more about Wallis Simpson, there's a section of books on her and The Duke of Windsor in the library."

"This isn't the library?" Wallis asked.

The girl laughed. "No, this is just a lounge. We have a beautiful big library across the quad. Would you like me to take you there?"

"Thank you. I know where it is," said Heather.

Wallis looked up at the girl and said, "Thanks."

"You know, you look like Wallis when she was young." She held the photo next to Wallis' face. "You really do. Lucky you. She was a beautiful woman." Then she smiled and said, "Have a nice day," and walked away.

"Wallis, I think this is enough," said Heather.

"No. This is my only chance to know everything. Take me to the library."

As Heather led Wallis outside and down the long concrete stairs to the quad, Wallis stumbled twice and had to grab the rail. Her head was down. She said nothing about the beautiful modern campus that Oldfields had become. She seemed to be in a daze.

They entered the building. Heather stopped at the two large glass book displays before the library door. "These are books by or about Oldfields grads." She pointed to several books on the bottom shelf. "These three are about you."

Wallis bent over and stared for a moment. "May I see them?"

"There are more on the shelf inside."

They entered the glass door of the George A. Nevens Jr. Library. There were so many things a person from 1913 would have marveled at—beautiful carpeting, furniture, fluorescent lights, computers, the palladium windows with the view of the quad—but Wallis was quiet.

"The books are over here," said Heather, and Wallis

followed her to one of many neat stacks.

There were five books about the Duchess of Windsor on the upper shelf and five about the Duke of Windsor below. But what Wallis immediately gravitated to was the Time Magazine cover showing a full-body portrait of Wallis Simpson. The date was January 4, 1937. She turned it over and read the details. "Wallis Warfield Simpson, Woman of the Year." She turned to Heather and smiled. Heather nodded.

Wallis took the first book off the shelf.

"Why don't we go over here," said Heather as she directed her friend to an area with comfortable chairs. "Have a seat. I'll find a book for myself and join you."

When Heather returned with her book, Wallis was deep into hers. Sometimes Wallis would just make a statement. "My mother died in 1929." Or "All the places I went!" She spoke with a flatness such comments did not deserve.

Sometimes, she would whisper a question to Heather like, "Who were the Nazis?" which she pronounced *naz-zies*. And Heather would answer to the best of her ability.

"Did the world see us as Nazi allies?"

Heather demurred, "Many did… but you know, Edward's abdication may have saved England in the end."

Wallis would nod and return to her book.

"Why did the royal family hate us so?"

And Heather would try to provide a contextual answer.

"Do you think all we did was have a never-ending social life?"

And Heather would point to things the Duke and Duchess did that were viewed favorably by the ordinary world.

And Wallis would ask if Heather thought she could have had this affair and that affair. And Heather would say that some of these accounts were just gossip, but between the lines, Wallis read that many of these claims were likely true.

The afternoon wore on. Wallis refused to break for food. Heather was afraid to leave her alone.

Wallis would look up from a book with tears in her eyes. "I would not have done that." or "How could they say that?"

Each time she read an account of her treatment of the Duke of Windsor in their later years together in Paris, she stopped reading, closed her eyes, and shook her head. And Heather heard her mumble more than once, "I really was terrible to him at the end." And Heather would explain that Wallis was old, tired, and sick herself by this point.

And when she castigated herself for not being with her husband when he died—that he died in the arms of his nurse and not in *her* arms—Heather could say nothing.

When Wallis looked up from the last book, it was after 7 PM.

"We'd better get going," said Heather. "You can't

miss your train."

Wallis rose from the chair like a woman five times her age and followed her friend back from the library. She would lag behind Heather, and Heather would wait for her and put her arm around her.

"Better grab the rail," Heather said as they arrived at the stairs. "You can't afford to break an ankle or something."

Wallis looked at her, forced a smile, nodded, and grabbed the rail.

They arrived at Heather's dorm room in silence. Wallis began to change out of the clothing Heather gave her.

"No. No. Leave those on. You can't leave here in those bloomers or whatever you call them. I'll put your dress and other clothing in this bag to take with you. And I'll take a flashlight. It's getting dark."

Heather showed her how to turn the flashlight on. Wallis nodded, and they walked out together. When they arrived at Glencoe Road, Heather stopped; then Wallis stopped and faced her.

"I shouldn't have done this, should I?" Wallis asked.

"It's OK. You had to know."

"I'm a good person, aren't I?"

"If you weren't, you wouldn't be my best friend."

Through tears and smiles, they hugged. Heather turned on the flashlight and handed it to Wallis. Then Wallis began her walk to the train.

***

Miss Nan was at the train station, lantern in hand. Wallis ran into her arms.

"Miss Nan, you've got to help me. Heather was right. You were right. I shouldn't have done it. I should have listened."

Miss Nan raised her hand. "Let's talk and walk, dear."

They started back.

"I should have stayed with Heather. You'd show the letter to my mother, and she'd get over it eventually, and I would start my life over in 2020. "

"Listen to me, child. During the limited time one can travel, you are protected by a kind of envelope, if you will. You and everything with you are unchanged."

"Like Heather's phone."

"Yes. But that envelope eventually disappears. Staying with Heather in *her* time would not have been an option; let me dispel you of that notion. You would have died… When will you die, dear?"

"1986."

"So, if you had stayed in 2020 beyond the time allowed… "

"I would have become what I looked like thirty-four years after my death."

"And if you were with Heather, it would have been horrible for her to see."

"Oh my God. How awful!"

"Have you traveled this way, Miss Nan?"

"Yes. Many times."

"I'm not sure I'll be able to live like this—knowing when I'll be married and then divorced, then married again and divorced again. And the thought that I will be unhappy even after becoming a duchess."

"And before, you couldn't live without knowing."

"Can I change my future, Miss Nan?

"No, dear. I believe one's future is set."

"It's possible to get rid of these memories, then. You *must* have a way to do it."

"There is a way. But like time travel, it has many risks."

"What could happen?"

"It could take away more than you want. Your childhood. Growing up. Memories of your friends and relatives. Sometimes all."

"All? Everything?"

"Yes. It's tragic. And once they're gone, they're gone forever. Our memories are the bedrock of who we are."

Wallis began to cry.

"Now, now. I will tell you this. Over time, the bad memories fade—not disappear—but lessen, and the good ones remain and even augment. Can you live with that notion?"

"I think so... Miss Nan, I know you said my future can't be changed. But maybe if I really put my mind to it."

"Oh, Wallis! I guess if anyone could do it, it would be you."

"You know, Mary has always been my best friend."

"Yes."

"But… "

"But you felt something special with Heather."

"Yes, and… "

"And as you move forward with your life, you would really like to have Heather there."

"Yes. That's it. Not that Mary wouldn't be, but Heather…"

"Understands. Especially now."

"Yes. I guess what I would wish above all else is a way to stay in touch with her. I was thinking: I know the train carries mail; I see them load it at the stations. But could the special trains carry mail too?"

"Wallis dear. I'm afraid that just can't be. But there is something else. Come here."

Miss Nan put down the lantern and placed her hands on the sides of Wallis' head. A moment later, Wallis jumped back with the flash and shock. "Ow! Miss Nan, what was that?"

"Don't ask me to explain it, dear. Suffice to say it will enable you and Heather to communicate?"

"Communicate? How?"

"In your dreams. I did the same thing to Heather."

"You did it to Heather?"

"Just before she left. And she was none too pleased."

"I'll bet she had a few choice words."

"Yes. A few… Wallis, I will be here for you as long as I am alive."

Wallis started to cry.

"You saw that awful painting of me, didn't you?"

"The one with you knitting?"

"Yes. I don't know why I agreed to pose for that. Why couldn't it be me with my students?"

Wallis laughed, then became quiet.

"Are you thinking of the inscription, dear?"

"Yes."

"That I'll die in 1928?"

"Oh, Miss Nan, life is so sad."

"Do you remember the rest of it?"

"No."

"That I'll also be with my girls until the end. That's fifteen more lovely years. And now, you'll also have Heather as a friend to go through life with."

Wallis and Miss Nan looked at each other and smiled.

Wallis picked up the lantern. "Race you back."

"Wallis Warfield, have you finally lost your mind?"

Of Flagpoles and Fireflies

In 1896, Simon Blodgett was born in the village of Warren, Maryland, nestled on the banks of the Gunpowder River. It produced the cotton duck that went into the sailcloth used by ships throughout America. Like other mill towns, Warren was built for the mill and was its own self-contained world.

Warren had the things you would want in any town—churches, stores, a blacksmith, a school, gyms for boys and girls, a community hall, a gristmill, a slaughterhouse, a sawmill, a library, a wheelwright, a shoemaker, and a doctor. There was the Odd Fellows and the Boy Scouts. There was a band. There were outings on the Fourth of July and turkeys for Christmas. Journeying outside of Warren was difficult.

Warren Elementary was the town's only school, offering grades one through eight. Simon graduated from Warren Elementary to a job in the mill. He was made the blacksmith's apprentice two years later and took over three years after that when the smithy died after a horse kick to the head. He was the only child of William and Louisa, who had worked in the mill since Simon's age. They lived in a stone tenement house they rented from Summerfield Baldwin, the man who owned the mill and most of the village.

Simon's home was warm and comfortable. Meals were always hot and filling. His mother would help him with his schoolwork and never missed a chance to give him a hug. Her embrace would take him into her world of cotton dyes, apple pies, and beef stew. He'd inhale, gathering all the emanations before her hug would force out his air. And there was no doubt she savored his aromas of steel, coal, and manure. His father taught him how to use his hands. A firm handshake from his father for a job well done was always followed with a smile and embrace. His father smelled of iron and oil.

He excelled at sports and all things physical. Simon had enough energy for any two people, and his enthusiasm for life spread to those around him. Everyone liked Simon.

On at least four occasions in the first grade, he was caught climbing the school flagpole and was sent to the principal's office. When asked why he did it, he said, "Have you seen the view? It's beautiful. You can see the bridge, the river, and the mill. You should try it." He was never punished.

On the contrary, when the rope got stuck in the rusty pulley, they called on Simon. When the wind twisted the flag so badly around the pole it couldn't be lowered at day's end, they summoned Simon. He graduated from *flag-fixer* to *flag-master*, a title he awarded himself when the principal gave him the honor of raising and lowering the flag each day. Simon took the work seriously as he did everything else. Instead of becoming vexed at the finicky fifty-five-foot pole, he relished any opportunity for a climb.

Years out of school, Simon, now a strapping young man, would still be asked from time to time to fix the challenging problems. He was happy for any excuse to shimmy up the wooden pole that now swayed more under his weight. If the pulley needed fixing, he'd take it off and repair it at the blacksmith shop. He set a high bar for future flag-masters.

Simon met Rose Hurst as students at Warren Elementary School. She left the village to attend Sparks High School, graduating in 1913. Sparks was the nearest town with a high school—five miles away and a full day's trip by horse and cart. She was fortunate to have an aunt and uncle in Sparks with whom she could stay. Rose was back home that first summer, working at the mill when she and Simon began seeing each other. He suggested lunch at the flagpole, and it became their daytime meeting place. Evenings were spent strolling by the river, taking dance lessons, or enjoying a movie at the community hall.

Everything about Rose was rosy. Her hair was strawberry blond, her skin was fair, her lips a deep pink, and she had a natural blush that always made Simon smile. Rose's ribbons and dresses all had something of her name. She loved art and wanted above all to be a teacher. This was no small feat for a mill girl, even though her father was a supervisor. Her letters to Simon were decorated with flowers and hearts. Later, she replaced her signature with a rose done in colored pencil.

In the warm summer evenings, there were fireflies—that's what Simon called them. She preferred to call them lightning bugs. Rose loved lightning, and lightning bugs were always around her. Simon once tried to brush them away, and she grabbed his wrist.

"No, I like them," she said.

"Why?" he asked.

And her answer made him fall in love with her: "They're like earth-bound stars." Simon was above all a practical young man and knew the fireflies were drawn by the lantern, but he liked her answer infinitely more. Even in the dusk, they would illuminate her face with their pulsating soft light.

Once, she asked him how he would describe the firefly's light. He stammered to give the correct answer: "Yellow—no—green!"

"Not the color, silly."

"… dim?"

"You're hopeless," she said, laughing.

"What is it then?"

"Patient. It's a patient light. It's in no hurry. Like the twinkling of a star."

It was indeed a patient light. Simon remembered such a light when he went with his father to the docks of Baltimore, the only time he left Warren. That night, in the distance, he saw a lighthouse for the first time.

He began seeing fireflies added to the flora of her letters.

Rose completed her Teaching Certificate in 1917, first in Baltimore, then in Towson when the Maryland State Normal School relocated there. Both Baltimore and Towson were too far to commute, and she found affordable rooms to rent. Again, her relationship with Simon had to be a summer one. When she finally returned to Warren for good, this hometown girl was immediately offered a job at the Warren School. She and Simon began to talk about their future. They had waited five years for each other. This mill town of nine hundred citizens assumed Simon and Rose would be married in short order. The outside world had other ideas.

The US declared war on Germany on April 6, 1917. In September, Simon was drafted and left for training at Camp Meade, Maryland. He was on a ship to France by July the following year, assigned to the 313th Infantry Regiment, *Baltimore's Own*, under Colonel Claude B. Sweezey. He arrived at the Western Front on September 12, 1918, as part of the Meuse-Argonne Offensive.

After an overnight artillery barrage, Simon's regiment fixed bayonets and marched out under a smoke-screen sent out by the gas and flame regiment. They traversed *No Man's Land*, made hell on earth by the shell craters and twisted barbed wire of four years of war. In the Malancourt Woods, they met withering resistance. Simon, always a good shot, was able to eliminate two snipers; and, at significant personal risk, saved six of his comrades who were pinned down by machine-gun fire while sustaining multiple wounds himself. Their prize, the strategic town Montfaucon, was captured on September 27. He was awarded the Distinguished Service Cross for extreme gallantry on the battlefield.

While American soldiers waged war in France, Rose was also fighting for her life. As Simon was recovering from his wounds in a French hospital, he received a long-delayed letter from his parents. On October 19, Rose had died of the Spanish Flu. He had not been at her bedside. He had not been there for her funeral. Although he missed his parents, he no longer had a reason to rush home. His spirit felt as desolate as No Man's Land.

The Armistice was signed on November 11. He stayed on until June of the following year to enforce it.

Simon came home a different man, a man changed by war and the loss of the woman he was to spend the rest of his life with. The hero's welcome planned by the village was postponed indefinitely.

He returned to work alongside Jimmy Smith, his former apprentice. He reclaimed his old bedroom at home. There was a haze over everything. His parents tried to be supportive. Speaking of Rose or the war was forbidden.

Months later, Simon was invited to the Hurst home following church. They shared photos of Rose— one of which was Rose with Simon, picnicking on the Gunpowder River. Beneath each timid smile, he sensed the *What ifs* and the *If onlys*. As he was leaving, Rose's mother handed him the letters her daughter had received from him—all wrapped in a bow. On top was the unsealed letter she had planned to mail when she became ill. Although Simon would see Rose's family many times throughout the year, handing him the letters signaled their way of moving on—something he was unprepared to do.

Rose was buried in the cemetery of Warren Methodist Episcopal Church, the same church Simon attended with his parents. He would visit her grave before or after Sunday services. On occasion, he would see her parents there, and they would greet each other with uneasy smiles and nods.

In late 1919, Simon's father collapsed at work and died of a suspected heart attack; his mother Louisa in 1920 of certain grief. Simon gave the eulogies for each.

He continued at the mill until it closed in 1922. Warren, and neighboring Bosley, had been bought by the City of Baltimore. The towns would be razed and flooded by the end of the same year to become the new Loch Raven Reservoir, providing the burgeoning city a source of clean drinking water. Everyone swore they'd never go to the new reservoir, even though there would be fishing and boating.

The Warren Methodist Episcopal Church, his church, was among the casualties of the flooding. He assisted in the difficult task of exhuming those buried in its cemetery for reburial in the Poplar Methodist Protestant cemetery to the east. Simon made sure extra care was given to Rose and to his parents; he personally reset the headstones.

He had arranged Rose's letters chronologically, interleafing those he had received with those he had written. It became his nightly routine to read some of them before drifting off to a fitful sleep— every letter except the one that was unsent.

Tonight, nearly six years after her passing, would be the night he opened her last letter.

He ate some dinner then washed his hands, arms, face, and chest. He changed into a clean shirt. He sat down again at the tiny table in his room, then got up again to bring over the lamp from his bedside.

The letter was still atop the same pile that he had read so many times. The envelope was face down, the flap open at a thirty-degree angle. He could see the top of the folded letter inside and could just make out the way the paper was embossed on the other side from the force of the pen. He took a breath and reached for the letter.

The first thing he noticed was the drawing. A large bouquet of roses set at the bottom of the letter with vines winding their way along both margins, much more elaborate than any previous letter. There was a single firefly. He noticed that the hand was shaky—not the bold loopy upright strokes he knew so well. Sentences sunk downwards as they approached the end of each line. Some *i*'s were un-dotted. Some *t*'s were uncrossed.

Dearest Simon,

The doctor is certain I have the Spanish Flu. As I write this, my parents are getting ready to take me to the infirmary.

Warren is so proud of you for your bravery in the war. No one is prouder than I am.

I was so relieved that you would be coming home at last.

I can't wait to see you.

I miss you so much.

When I recover, we'll commence where we left off.

You are and will always be my hero.

With much love,

Your Rose

He read through the letter again. He felt the words with the tips of his fingers. He brought the letter to his face and inhaled, hoping for her scent. He touched the bouquet and ran his finger over each stem, petal, and vine. He noticed that it was drawn in dark shades of brown, red, and green—not Rose's usual pastel palette. There were ribbons and bows in odd places. As he scanned over the bouquet once more, he thought he saw an *I* then the word *sign*. He pulled the lamp closer and, with the light from behind, was able to convince himself that Rose had written more, then decided to conceal it with a drawing.

He turned the letter over and, lightly running his fingertips over the area, could feel the words in the area of the bouquet. In the bottom drawer of his small desk, he found the tracing paper Rose had given him in her attempt to get him interested in art. He placed the paper over the back of the bouquet and, using the lightest back and forth strokes of a pencil, resurrected the writing in reverse. Holding it up to a mirror, he read:

I will do all I can to come home to you, my dearest. But the Flu has taken many lives, including three from our little town.

Know that I will always be waiting for you at our special place.

I promise you a sign.

With <u>everlasting</u> love,

Your Rose

He copied every word onto a clean sheet of paper, making sure he got it all right. *Why had she decided to cover this up? Why didn't she want me to see this?*

It was only when he read it through again to check his copy, he noticed that *everlasting* had been underlined. He carefully added the detail.

He poured himself a glass of water and drank it slowly, eyes fixed straight ahead toward the window without looking at it. Simon smiled when the answer came to him. *She wanted me to move on with my life.* He nodded. *That was it. That was so like her.*

But he knew moving on with another woman would be impossible.

He read the letter through again and began to cry. He reached into his pocket and blotted his eyes with the handkerchief. As he lowered it, he was aware of a faint light coming from the window—a single firefly on the glass.

He would have to make sure not to miss the sign.

Their special place had always been the tiny grassy area at the base of the school flagpole. The flagpole had been left standing after Warren had been dismantled and inundated, the only remains of his hometown still visible. He had made his way to the bank of the reservoir closest to the flagpole that stood defiantly a hundred feet away. *That damned pole! I should have chopped that son-of-a-bitch down when the rest of Warren was destroyed. It's like a middle finger sticking out of the water meant for me.* He often thought about finding a boat and bringing a saw to do the job himself. Then he just thought of getting a boat and going out to the pole. *Maybe the pole was the sign—or part of the sign—that he pledged to himself not to miss. It had to mean something. Why else would it be all that remained?* Then he understood the pole was the only tangible connection to the world he loved.

Simon needed a boat. He asked everyone who came into the Cockeysville blacksmith shop where he now worked. He asked Mrs. Barlowe, the widow who owned the small farmhouse where he paid for a room, the nearest place he could find to where Warren once stood.

The ancient rowboat belonged to an old farmer who could no longer remember how he came to have it. It was about as close to not being a boat while still being one. He sold it to Simon for a dollar—Simon insisting the price include transportation to his place using the farmer's horse and cart.

He smoothed the roughest places and patched the areas that looked like they might leak. The rusty oarlocks and splintery oars were serviceable with a bit of filing and sanding. There was no urgent need for paint. He got permission from Mrs. Barlowe to cut a trail from her property to the water. The following Sunday, after church and a visit to Rose's grave, he dragged the boat to the water and launched it—with extra caulking and a bailing bucket onboard. He sat in the boat and watched. To his surprise, the old wreck did not leak. After fifteen minutes, he rowed to the flagpole.

It had been over a year since the flooding, but the pole above the waterline was surprisingly intact. He ran his hand along the same wood that he had climbed so many times. The top pulley twenty feet above him appeared to be rusted. He pulled down on the rope, and it moved. He pulled again and again as the wet algae-covered rope rose from the water and over the pulley. Fortunately, the rope's end was not tied to the flagpole cleat. Then came into view the snap hooks onto which he had attached the American flag. He stopped. How many times on a windy day had he been wrapped in that flag! The new flag-master found this experience frightening. Simon had found comfort in it— embraced by the flag he loved, of the country he loved, in the place he and Rose loved.

He ran the rope for its entire length. Then he returned to shore. He covered the boat with branches, even though he was sure no one would come this way.

On Monday, he added a cleat to the bow of the boat. The following Sunday, he rowed again to the pole. He brought sandpaper, work gloves, tool-belt, oilcan, rags, hammer, nails, and rope. He lashed the boat tightly to the pole. He stood up, knees bent, the craft rocking crazily as he willed himself to slow down the pendulum movements of his legs and hips. He placed one gloved hand then the next on the pole, and in one motion, transferred his weight. Even though he was a blacksmith and very strong, he was surprised at how hard it was to hold on. By the time he focused, he had allowed himself to slip down. When he felt the cold water rush into his shoes, he reflexively bent his knees and withdrew his feet from the wet; then began with great difficulty to make his way up the pole.

When he arrived at the top pulley, he gripped tighter with his legs, located the sandpaper, and removed as much rust as he could before feeling a piercing burn in his thighs. He squirted oil on the pulley and, with great relief, made his way down the pole, acquiring splinters along the way. He lowered himself cautiously into the boat. He ran the rope and, upon reaching the snap hooks, sanded and oiled them. Finally, he hammered a huge nail into the pole above the waterline.

Why he wanted to do all this, he didn't know. He did know this pole would never fly a flag again.

Simon returned to shore. He would have spent the rest of the day in bed had he not been invited to join

Mrs. Barlowe for dinner. After dinner, she helped him remove those splinters he could not get to himself.

The following Monday, he affixed a metal loop and a weight to the wooden frame of the slate he used in elementary school. Every evening after dinner, he stared at the slate, chalk in hand. It was always blank when he turned off the lamp and went to sleep.

Sunday, he was back at the pole with the slate. He lashed the boat. He sat with the chalk in one hand and the slate in the other, thinking. With dusk and the first drops of rain, he clenched his teeth and wrote on the slate in block letters. He pulled on the rope until the clip rose within reach, then clipped on the slate. He paused to read the "I LOVE YOU" as it entered the water, then continued to lower it until it stopped. He tied the end of the rope around the pole and nail.

The following Sunday, after visiting the graves of Rose and his parents, he attended services. He was invited to join the Hursts for Sunday dinner but begged off, saying he was too tired. He went immediately to the pole. He untied the rope and closed his eyes as he hoisted up the rope. When he heard the sound of the slate breaking the water, he took a deep breath, held it, and opened his eyes. "I LOVE YOU." At first, he thought it was Rose's—but it was in his hand. *Why am I doing this? Do I really think something could happen? What if someone saw me?* Simon knew no one would see him. Not here. He hurriedly released the rope, allowing the slate to sink to the bottom, tied the rope off, and headed home.

The following Sunday, Simon was relieved to find it storming so much it would be impossible to go out. He had been thinking about what to write next. He reread Rose's last letter, again and again, spending the day in bed. The next workweek, like all before, was spent in a fog. He did his work, but just. He treated his customers with respect, but there was no superfluous conversation. He was adrift.

But by the following Thursday, the people around him were relieved to see him getting back to himself. He smiled and made a few jokes. He talked about the unusual heat and the deplorable condition of the roads.

That Sunday, he didn't attend church. He waited until dusk.

He found himself alone in the cemetery. He visited his parents and, after spending much less time than usual, slinked away as if he had done a shameful thing. As he came to Rose's headstone, he felt the first drops of rain. He looked at the sky and saw billowing grey clouds. He removed his hat and got down on his knees.

"Mom and Dad are gone. You are gone. I came home from that horrible war to be with you. I came back to an empty home, an empty life, a life without you, Rose.

"How do you expect me to go on? I've looked for the sign. I can't find it. I'm so sorry. This is the only way I can be with you."

He removed the pistol—his father's pistol—from his jacket pocket. As he raised the barrel to his head, the rain came down harder. His hand trembled as he cocked the hammer. He stared straight ahead at the headstone.

ROSE MARIE HURST
BORN MAY 14, 1896
DIED OCTOBER 19, 1918
A SHINING STAR FOREVER IN OUR HEARTS

The fireflies came in a swarm and covered the stone around her name. Their lights, at first blinking randomly, became one. More replaced those knocked off the stone by the pounding raindrops. Those washed to the ground flew or crawled back up the stone to take their place with the others.

Fireflies in a thunderstorm? He looked around him. They were only on Rose's stone. He lowered the pistol, uncocked the trigger, and put the gun in his belt. The fireflies rose from the stone en masse and headed south as he quickly got to his feet. In the darkness, they lit his way to the boat. Then he was on the water. The flagpole covered in fireflies was now a beacon in the gathering storm. He saw the lightning to his southwest getting closer. He lashed the boat to the pole. The flagpole rope slapped the pole angrily.

Lightning struck the water fifty feet away and caused the plant life beneath the surface to ignite and extinguish with crackles and puffs. The pole was trembling with a current that surged through his body as he untied the rope, then gripped it and pulled down, gripped and pulled down again, and then again until he heard the clack of wood hitting metal. He looked up to the top of the pole and saw the slate, its frame bristling with sparks. His eyes strained through the pelting rain but couldn't read it. He released the rope to lower it; it was stuck. He climbed the pole. When he reached the top, he wiped his eyes and focused on the slate.

In large white letters, the word "COME."

The lightning was getting closer with each strike. Thunderclaps sounded like the splitting of giant trees. The lightning bugs fled as their namesake pushed away all other nature from the night. As the lightning struck the water around him, he saw its tendrils spread like a web.

Each jagged electric tear in the fabric of the black sky sent fingers into the water, and the world beneath would illuminate for an instant. He saw an amber-infused Warren—the view from the top of the flagpole—the bridge, the river, and the mill. Simon removed the pistol from his belt, fired its single bullet into the boat's floor, and then tossed in the gun. As it landed, it was struck by a blinding bolt of lightning followed by exploding wooden shards. Simon gripped the pole with his legs and shielded his eyes.

He made his way down the vibrating pole, clenching closed his eyelids. The next strike hit the slate at the top of the pole, exploding the metal into molten slag. He untied the rope at the waterline. As he continued downward and the water reached his chin, he took his deepest breath and held it. Then he went under.

The thunder hushed. The lightning through his eyelids became the soft patient pulsing of the firefly. His knee-grip relaxed with each hand over hand, then tightened again. The pole swayed in the water. The vegetation slapped his hands and face as the light dimmed and the sounds grew faint. Then came the heavy slipperiness of silt that resisted his kicking feet. As he pushed himself deeper, the mire pressed with increasing force against his face. It entered his nose and ears. He was drowning. Then he thought of the slate and forced himself downward again. He blew the silt from his nose and pushed himself down in yet another stride.

Suddenly, his feet felt as if they had been released from quicksand. He forced himself down once more and knew that his lower body was free. He perceived a brightening through his eyelids and a rumble in his ears. As he pushed himself lower once more, he found himself released from the water's weight. In hard gasps, he filled his lungs with air. He wiped the mud from his face and looked down.

Below him, laughing, crying, and waving, stood Rose and next to her, his parents. Behind them were the people of Warren.

Banners read "WELCOME HOME SIMON" and "OUR HERO." The Warren Band played.

Simon was home.

The Amazingest Dog of Baltimore County

Margaret Brooks looked older than her forty-eight years—mostly from sun exposure and partly from an aversion to cosmetics. She lived in a small house that had once been the servants' quarters before the farm was divided. Her modest acre sat in the distant corner of a modern farm that raised feed corn and dabbled in a rare breed of cattle. From her kitchen window, she could see the remains of the foundation of the original grand house amidst the fragrant honeysuckle, lilac, and azalea. Mature trees lined both sides of the dirt road that led to her home. It looked like rural France except for the denouement at the road's end.

The first of her Brooks family line came to Baltimore County in 1660. She and her brother Philip were the last ones. Whereas Margaret knew exactly where she came from, the pup was a different story.

In a fit of loneliness, she decided to stop by an animal shelter to adopt a cat, one that was older and preferably neglected—in other words, she wanted a creature like her—and one that could be her friend. Most importantly to her, the shelter was a no-kill facility, and for that alone, it was worth the extra forty-minute drive and the cost of gas, which of late was eighteen cents a gallon higher than usual.

She was shown around by Trina, an amiable pudgy Goth, and recent hire. Trina remarked how unusual it was to have no cats. There were always cats. It was dogs they sometimes ran out of.

"Maybe I'll just have a look around," Margaret said.

Margaret looked into all the cages. She was on the verge of leaving when she spotted the pup, alone and shivering in his cage on the floor in the far corner of the room. The place was warm enough; he wasn't shivering from the cold. As she painfully squatted, he retreated to the far end of the cage and stared at her—giant white rims around his irises—*whale eye*—a sign of fear. His pointy ears were pinned back—another sign. Margaret noticed his water bowl and food were untouched.

She put the back of her hand against the bars. The dog slowly extended his neck and took a single sniff, then pulled back. Margaret kept her hand there, wiggling her fingers, so they barely tapped the cage and whispered, "Hi there, cutie." She knew to avert her gaze as the pup took one tiny plodding step after another until he reached her. When he licked her fingers, she felt a chill. She got down on her hands and knees and looked into his eyes. He pressed hard against the bars until they indented his mushy black nose. To her own surprise, she did the same and was rewarded with a lick on her nose, then another and another. When she began to cry, Trina ran over and helped her to her feet.

"What's his name?" Margaret asked, drying her eyes in embarrassment.

"He doesn't have a name yet. He was just dropped off yesterday. He was left in a box by the door during the night. Would you like to see him?"

A moment later, Margaret was holding him in her hands. She lowered him to the floor. His small, jittery steps left tracks of wet sawdust. She first noticed the out-sized paws and long black legs, then the belly with the black extending onto the front of his neck and under his chin—something both Margaret and Trina remarked they had never seen before. The rest of his body and face were white with brown patches. His muzzle was fine but a little long; his eyes were round, deep, and brown. His long tail set plastered between his legs.

"What breed do you think he is?" Margaret asked.

Trina shrugged. "He looks a bit like a Jack Russell— in the upper half anyways."

"The bottom half looks like it walked through a tar pit," quipped Margaret. They both laughed then Margaret caught herself. Margaret was a skinny long-legged teen and, coupled with her shyness and ordinary looks, was on the receiving end of a slew of unflattering nicknames.

Spider-girl was their favorite. On the track team, the coach called her *Stretch*. She looked at the pup and thought, *I'm sorry, honey. It will never happen again.* And it didn't.

It turned out Trina was partially correct. His

mother was a show-quality Great Dane by the name of "Merryman Sleeping Beauty," and his father was a Jack Russell named Peter—a.k.a. "Sneaky Pete." While Sleeping Beauty—massively in heat with her pheromones wafting across the county—awaited the attentions of her planned breeding partner Ch. Fairdale Sir Archibald, who was being schlepped in at great expense from PA, she decided to take a beauty nap. All it took was one whiff, and SP was in lust.

He bolted from his farm three miles north and made it to his paramour in record time. A veteran of many agility competitions, he would have customarily cleared the five-foot chain-link fence with ease; but he didn't account for the huge erection that nearly turned him from hurdler into pole-vaulter. He managed to make a quick mid-air adjustment, twisting his body in a variant of the Fosbury Flop, and landed inside her enclosure cat-like, on all fours. Fortunately for Pete, Sleeping Beauty was bred for beauty, not brains, and he had his way with her before it registered that it wasn't her own tail *back there*. Due to the difference in the sizes of their relevant anatomy, locking wasn't an issue, and after a running start and a step on her haunches to give him some extra clearance, he was back over the fence and home in time for lunch. Archie would be stuck with sloppy seconds.

Two months later, the litter of eleven was born— most of them already promised or sold. The gist of what happened was apparent. The bitch's owners euthanized the pups, and the fence was promptly raised to seven feet. Correction: they euthanized all but one of the pups. The runt had crept away and was picked up by a Good Samaritan hiking in the nearby woods.

Margaret fell head-over-heels for the dog and brought him home as soon as he had his shots. She decided for some reason—*She had a feeling*—not to have him neutered, above the objections of the shelter staff.

She named the pup Davis. It was a perfect name and the absolutely right thing to do. Davis Brooks was her favorite uncle. Like her, he had lived alone and preferred it that way. He died when his cabin caught fire the previous year, likely from smoking in bed. She attended the small funeral and said a few words but always wanted to do more for the man who taught her to fish and be independent. Somehow the pup reminded her of her uncle.

Davis grew quickly—at least his legs did. Dr. Grey, the vet whose practice was mainly large animals and was not known for sensitivity, joked that the dog reminded him of a Humvee or a scissors lift and assured Margaret that the rest of him would catch up, eventually. She bit her lip and made a mental note not to send him a Christmas card.

Davis did sort of grow into his legs. Otherwise, he turned out to be the best his parents' breeds had to offer. He was not only bright and athletic but mellow and sweet. Margaret and Davis became inseparable, and he had the sense to never be underfoot, something she could not tolerate in a dog.

Margaret had fished the Gunpowder her entire life.

But it wasn't her passion. Margaret had no passions. As an adult, fishing was a relaxing thing to do on a nice day.

When winter appeared to finally be over, she'd bring her two fly boxes by the Great Feathers Fly Shop where Ted, a long-time employee, would see what was missing and fill in the gaps.

There would be small talk. "Looks like you went to town on them Light Cahills last year," he would say. And she would say something like, "Mostly, it was the trees that got 'em." And after a bit of back and forth, he would say, "This the year you finally decide to learn to tie a few, hon?" And she would say, "Not this year, Ted. Too much to do—and besides, you need the business."

The truth was that Ted, a widower, had a thing for Margaret, and she had a sense of it, but a relationship was just not on her to-do list.

Now that it was warming up, Margaret made her annual pilgrimage to the fly shop, boxes in hand, with Davis in tow. The door opened with a jingle. A smiling Ted appeared from the back room. "Margaret!"

"Hi, Ted!"

Davis barked, wagged, and ran immediately over to Ted, who bent over to pet him. Ted's own dog, an old Yellow Lab named Missy, came over to see what all the commotion was. She met Davis in the usual way, then went over to Margaret for a rub.

"Who do we have here, Margaret?"

"My new dog. His name is Davis."

"Davis, eh. After your uncle?"

"Yep."

"What breed is he?" he said jokingly.

"Curbstone Setter. Purebred." She smiled, and they both laughed.

"Lemme get a look at you, boy." He stepped back to have a better look. "Planning on taking him fishing?"

"I guess so. He comes with me everywhere."

"By the looks of him, I think he may be a great fishing dog. The weather should hold out. People are doing well with stonefly imitations."

She smiled and held out the two fly boxes. Ted opened them and smiled. "Looks like you went to town on them Light Cahills."

During his early morning walk, Margaret said to Davis, "Wanna go fishing today, boy?" He wagged and barked like she had never heard him before.

This season, fishing would take on new importance. Her inheritance gone and savings drying up, Margaret was toying with the idea of getting a job somewhere just to cover utilities, gas money, and incidentals. Her house was paid off, thank God, but was perpetually in need of repair. The few she couldn't manage herself were always expensive. Her vegetable garden was pretty productive… but what about a protein source? Jimmy Randolph wasn't deer hunting anymore, so there was no trading meat for vegetables. It would have to be fish.

They headed for Bluemount Rd.

They entered the water near the parking lot. Although the bank was muddy, the water was calm and the footing secure. Davis walked in cautiously. He yelped and jumped two feet out of the water when he saw his reflection. Margaret laughed, gave him a quick head-rub, and he knew everything was OK.

He watched Margaret and the other fishermen and the happiness they experienced when they brought fish out of the water. Davis exuberantly went after the fish himself but soon learned that all the splashing chased them away. She gave him the sign to settle down, and he did.

He walked about ten feet upstream. Then, in short order, two amazing things happened. First, he would slowly allow his legs to bend, and he would sink under-water. Margaret could see from his protruding ears that he was scanning underwater for fish until he locked on. Then—Amazing Thing Number Two—he would slowly raise his head from the water, then his body, and point toward the fish. But *Jack Danes*, not innately pointers, do it their own way. He brought his right paw out of the water and extended his *index finger*.

After Margaret raised her fallen jaw, she casted beyond the target and let her fly drift downstream toward where he had pointed. A moment later, she was rewarded with a strike—a beautiful young Rainbow. As she netted it, Davis came in for a closer look. He sniffed the flopping fish and then looked at Margaret, who beamed at him. He knew he had done well.

She released the fish. As they moved upstream, they had success after success. On the eighth or ninth time, she kept him close and verified what she suspected. Before each repositioning of his submerged head, there would be a faint stream of bubbles coming from his nose. Yes, he was sniffing for the fish's scent! She couldn't imagine an ordinary dog willingly allowing water up his snout, but Davis was not ordinary. He apparently prioritized finding fish and thus pleasing Margaret above the discomfort. That made Amazing Thing Number Three.

Margaret, always a private person, decided not to publicize Davis' skills, and fly fishing, a private sport, was ideal for keeping her secret.

They packed up and headed to the part of the river south of Corbett where they could keep the fish. Margaret parked in what was barely a pull-off, known only to locals when Amazing Thing Number Four happened. He ran ahead of her before she could enter the water. He stepped in, and when his body was underwater, poked his head under and had a look around, then turned to face her as if to say the coast was clear. She entered six feet to his left. He growled, and moments later, she was in up to her neck. Margaret knew enough not to panic; she threw her rod to the bank and swam out safely. But from then on, she let him pick the way in.

They caught the five trout limit within an hour and headed home. That evening, Davis had his first trout dinner.

When she wasn't fishing, she was expanding her vegetable garden. She rented a farm-stand from an old friend and opened it on weekends selling fresh vegetables and fish. In two years, she replenished her savings account.

With Margaret's success came a new self-assurance and, with that, happiness. For the first time in her life, she thought about what it would be like to share it with someone. Ted came immediately to mind. She found herself in the fly shop more and more. Their conversations migrated from fishing to what everyone called small talk. A month later, he suggested they meet for coffee at that new place people was talking about, The Filling Station.

She had driven by this former gas station, now coffee and sandwich shop, on her way to her farm-stand. They decided to take a chance and try the exotic-sounding *cappuccino* for the first time, and they enjoyed it a lot. They agreed it must be what it's like to sip coffee in Italy.

After a year, they were married in a quiet civil ceremony. Ted sold his house and moved in with Margaret and Davis. They were both supremely happy, as were Davis and Missy, Ted's dog. Soon enough, Margaret took Ted fishing, and what he saw beat the hell out of any cappuccino. That's all he could talk about—to Margaret only. She swore him to silence and, at the risk of losing an important body part. He complied.

Davis' birthday was a quiet celebration featuring dog food molded into a cake shape, with a single candle on top. After Ted and Margaret sang Happy Birthday, Davis was encouraged to blow out the candles. He was a smart dog but not smart enough to grasp the concept. Ted brought in a wrapped rawhide bone. Davis went nuts and had the paper off in seconds. With the bone in his mouth, he watched Margaret open his second gift. This may have been the first time in history a dog received swim goggles for his birthday.

"Whatya think, boy?" she said as she dangled them in front of his eyes. He dropped the bone and sniffed. "Wanna try them on?" she asked. He said nothing. "You do?" she said as if he really answered her in the affirmative.

She made a few adjustments, held them to his face, and made a few more. She stretched the rubber straps and maneuvered them on. He shook his head, and the goggles flew across the room. There were two more attempts with the same results until Ted suggested a little food reward which did the trick for a couple of minutes.

"Let's leave the boy alone, Margaret. It's his birthday, after all."

"You're right. We'll give it another go at the river."

Margaret prided herself on how she chose her flies. Unlike many fisher-people who would tie on a fly in the parking lot, she would wait until she got into the river to see what was in the air and in the water. It was not uncommon for her to turn over rocks looking for nymphs and the shucks of subaquatic insects the fish were feeding on that day. Davis would look and sniff as well.

The day after the big birthday celebration, Margaret and Ted stood in the middle of the stream, Ted there just to observe. Margaret got the goggles on Davis, and Ted rewarded him. The dog shook his head, but the goggles stayed put. Davis seemed to nod his acceptance, then lowered his chassis so his head was underwater. They saw him looking around. His tail-wagging sped to the point they thought he would take off like a motorboat. Vast streams of bubbles emitted from his muzzle, and as his head rose above the surface, he was barking wildly as if he had discovered the key to the dog food vault. Ted and Margaret gave him an enthusiastic rub, and he was off doing surveillance upstream.

Margaret and Ted's attention was drawn to the dozens of flies in her fly-box. As usual, Davis found a target and pointed. When Margaret's cast didn't follow, he looked back and, seeing what they were doing, walked back to them. She looked down at him. Then he reached up and placed his paw on her wrist. She lowered her hand and the box of flies. Then came Amazing Thing Number Five. He looked at each fly in the box, pointed at his choice, then looked up at her. With tears in her eyes, she looked at him and Ted. Ted was crying too. She tied that one on and cast where he pointed. They landed the biggest Brown she had ever seen.

Their five fish were caught in short order, and they headed back to the car. When Ted tried to remove the goggles, Davis growled and backed away. For some time after that, Ted called him The Red Baron.

Davis, a dog of unusual instincts, had all the usual ones as well. He had not been neutered and thus had the drive to reproduce. Fortunately for all concerned, they lived in a secluded area with no bitches in heat within sniffing distance. Davis seemed content humping the occasional leg or Missy. Missy was OK with the arrangement. Ted and Margaret thought about breeding Davis. They knew they'd outlive him and couldn't see life without a *Gunpowder River Pointer*, as they now referred to his breed in private.

They went online and looked at every breed there was. The vet suggested genetic testing to find out what he actually was. The truth surprised and didn't surprise them at the same time. It just made sense.

A month later, Missy died in her sleep. They buried her in the backyard. Davis attended the ceremony. He mourned his friend to the point of declining fishing trips. Davis was now moping more and more.

The situation became urgent when he stopped eating. Margaret made a trip to the shelter, praying there would be someone for Davis. An excited Trina directed her to bottom corner cage—Davis' cage. The cowering female pup had gangly dark legs and a brown and white body. Sneaky Pete had struck again.

Margaret asked that Trina hold the dog until Davis could visit. An hour later, Davis gave his enthusiastic approval. They named the bitch Mavis. It had been amazing that Davis had escaped demise, and it was miraculous that Mavis proved that lightning does sometimes strike twice in the same place.

Margaret and Ted forbade her getting spayed. After her shots, she was taken home and immediately became part of the family. In short order, Davis taught her everything about fishing. Margaret bought Mavis her very own goggles.

Davis and Mavis were bred. The litter of eight had all the desirable traits of their parents and no apparent medical problems. They were sold as Gunpowder River Pointers for exorbitant prices through a network more secretive than the Masons.

Margaret and Ted spent the rest of their long lives together fishing, fly tying, enjoying their dogs, friends, and family (in that order), vacationing in Maine, and trying new coffee drinks. They thought about a trip to Italy but didn't want to be away from Davis and Mavis. Instead, they watched a travelogue on Italy on their new sixty-inch high-definition TV while sipping their cappuccinos.

In other words: They lived happily ever after.

Epilogue

Did this story seem to end abruptly? Was the ending too "pat"?

My dear readers: It's not my fault.

It is a fact that writers get to know their characters like family members. What I didn't realize was that it also works in reverse. The more I wrote about Margaret, the more she knew about me. My story about Margaret and Davis was my fifth for a book of short stories. In a daydream, Margaret accused me of writing dark stories about unhappy or lonely people. "What happened to the fairy tale ending? That's all I want," she said. In the end, we came to an understanding. The last thing I wanted was to get into a fight with her (and Davis). God-forbid! What if I needed her help again? So I agreed.

How Fishing Almost Ruined My Life—and How A Man in a Can Saved It

I was an ordinary guy leading an ordinary life. I thought I was happy.

The day started off fine. I parked in the Monkton lot and walked north on the trail for a short distance, where I entered the river. I headed downstream, making short casts toward both banks. I had had a few nibbles. I changed flies. I took a glance back at the trees, but as soon as I back-casted, I knew I had too much line out. The forward cast stopped abruptly. I cursed under my breath as I turned around, expecting to see my line in a tree. Instead, it seemed to end in the bank. Not wanting to lose my carefully-tied Sulphur Wet, I made my way over to the bank.

My tippet protruded from what looked like a hole in the ground. As I got closer, I saw that my fly had somehow landed inside a mostly-buried beer can. What are the chances of that?

I pulled gently on the tippet; nothing budged.

I grabbed the rim of the can and rocked it back and forth to loosen it from the pebbly clay. The old can was heavy—at least ten pounds. *It must be loaded with sediment,* I thought. I turned it around. All I could read was "NAT" in white letters against red. The rest was various shades of rust. It did occur to me to just cut the tippet and be done with it.

I maneuvered the can onto a large flat rock and retrieved the pocketknife from my bag. I placed the blade's tip in the middle of the lid and pressed hard. There was a give as the point penetrated. Suddenly, I heard *from the can,* "JESUS CHRIST! NOW YOU DID IT! I'M BLEEDIN' HERE!"

I jumped back, dropping my knife. I took a deep breath and walked back to the can. I bent over and said, "Hello."

"HELLO YOURSELF, YOU MORON. GET ME OUTTA HERE!"

"Shhh. I'll get you out. I'll take you home. I have tools at home."

"JESUS CHRIST. HOW LONG WILL THAT TAKE?"

"Twenty minutes. Not long."

"NOT LONG FOR YOU! YOU'RE NOT IN A FUCKIN' CAN!"

"But you must have been in there a long time. Twenty minutes isn't very much, comparatively."

"WHO ARE YOU—FUCKIN' EINSTEIN? I WAS SLEEPING UNTIL YOU STABBED ME IN

THE HEAD."

"I apologize. This thing is pretty unusual, you have to admit."

"YOU PLAN TO KEEP BLABBIN' WHILE I BLEED TO DEATH?"

"Right. I'll have you out of there soon. I promise. I have a special can opener at home that—"

"JESUS. I'M SCREWED. OF ALL THE DAMN PEOPLE, I HAVE TO GET CHATTY CATHY."

"Right. Sorry."

I clipped the tippet and reeled in my line. With the rod under my arm, I squatted and lifted the can from the ground. Clutching it against my belly, I made my way back to the car. Whoever was in there was quiet, thank God, but the stench coming from the opening, was unbearable. I stopped and retched.

"WHY'D YOU STOP?"

"You stink."

"OF COURSE I DO, YOU IDIOT. YOU THINK *I* LIKE THIS? I WAS A TWO-SHOWER-A-DAY GUY. I WAS THE BEST-GROOMED DUDE IN ADVERTISING."

"You were in advertising?"

"WALK!"

We made it home. He was quiet except for the stream of expletives when the can slipped from my hands and dropped onto the floor of my trunk. I parked in the driveway. I opened the garage, quickly put away my fishing equipment, and backed out my wife's car. I placed the can in the middle of the garage floor and told him I'd be right back. My wife was already in the kitchen having coffee and reading the paper.

"Why are you back so early? Didn't you go fishing?"

In my haste to follow can-man's orders, I didn't think ahead to this scenario. She could sense I was preoccupied.

"Like a cup?" she asked, holding up hers.

"In a bit."

"Why are you in such a hurry?"

I sighed.

"What happened? Did you have an accident?"

"No."

"What is it, honey?"

"… I found this beer can."

"You found a beer can."

"A very heavy beer can."

"And you're in a hurry to get back to your heavy beer can."

"… Yes… Where's that new can opener? You know the one that opens cans from the side instead of the top."

"It's in the junk drawer on the right… Honey, were you out in the heat?"

I began rummaging in the drawer.

"No."

"Did you have something to eat before you left?"

"Yes. The usual."

I found the can opener and hurried back to the garage. As I knelt next to the can and fumbled to get the can opener in the proper position, my wife appeared at the garage door.

"What's that awful smell?"

"Don't worry. I'll spray."

I put my mouth near the can opening and whispered, "My wife is here. Don't say anything."

"Honey, are you talking to that can?"

"… Yeah, but I can ex—"

"Honey, don't worry, I'm just going inside for a moment—"

Before she got out an "I'll be right back," can-man said, "WHAT'S THE BITCH'S NAME?"

Silence and stillness, then tentatively, I said, "Jackie."

My wife was shaking as she said, "Did the can say that?"

" … Yes."

"And did it just call me a bitch?"

"YES, I DID. YOU DEAF TOO—BITCH?"

"WHY YOU ASSHOLE!" she exploded.

As I feebly said, "But he's been in a can for a very long time…" Jackie was flying toward the can and, with the form from her soccer days, kicked it with all her might—and expected it to sail into my tool wall. Instead, its dented form rolled a few feet as she screamed, falling to the floor and grabbing her right foot.

"SON-OF-A-BITCH! I THINK I BROKE MY FOOT!"

"GOOD! YOU KNOW WHAT, BITCH? YOU CRAZY!" came from the can.

"I told you… it was heavy." I whimpered.

"YOU'RE DEAD. CAN-MAN," screamed my bookish wife as she crawled on hands and knees to the can. Once over the lid, she added, "YOU HEAR ME, ASSHOLE! YOU'RE DEAD!"

With that, she lifted the can over her head and slammed it onto the concrete garage floor. On its way to the floor, I heard "SHIIIIT" coming from the can.

There was a deafening quiet as we looked on. The can had split in several places. All we saw inside was… black hair. Dirty black hair. I walked over to my wife, helped her up on her good foot, and put my arm around her shoulders. We looked at each other then back at the can. Then the can rocked and began prying itself open until it was flat against the floor—with a hairball in its center. Coming from the hairy mass were two small hands and two small feet. He was now upon its knees. Amid subdued *fucks, shits and damns*, he got to his feet. He turned in tiny steps to face us. Can-man was no more than eight inches tall. There was a spot of congealed blood on his crown. As his filthy hands parted his hair, he looked at us from a single, large round eye.

My wife was first to speak as she slowly got up on her left foot. "Listen to me, whatever you are."

"WHATEVER?" can-man said.

"SHUT UP, YOU. Now, this is the way it's going to be. Frank, you're going to get my old crutches from the hall closet, then you're going to hose *him* down."

"WHAT THE HELL HAPPENED TO YOUR

EYE?"

(Jackie wore an eye patch, the result of a childhood accident.)

"NONE OF YOUR BUSINESS, YOU HAIRY TURD."

"WHAT DID YOU CALL ME, CAPTAIN HOOK?"

"YOU DEAF, CAN-MAN?"

"YOU DON'T KNOW WHO I AM, DO YA, HON?"

"DON'T YOU *HON* ME, HAIRBALL. ALL I KNOW IS YOU BROKE MY FOOT, AND YOU'RE STINKIN' UP MY HOUSE."

"*I* BROKE YOUR FOOT? DID I ASK YOU TO KICK MY CAN?"

"YOU PROVOKED ME, NUMBNUTS."

"I'm going to get the crutches, OK? Then I'll come back and hose him off… and then do whatever you want me to, OK?"

She jerked my landscaping shovel from its clip.

"Better make it quick before I squash him."

She stood there facing him, like a soldier guarding a prisoner. They were frozen in the same position when I returned with the crutches. As I gave them to her, she handed me the shovel, which I dutifully clipped back to the garage wall tool rack.

"Hose him off, then drive me to urgent care," she said.

From the hair, which touched the ground, he stuck

out his right hand.

"Call me Nat," he said.

"I'm Frank, and this is Jackie, my wife," I said as I cautiously shook his tiny hand.

"Sorry I was so upset. Being stuck in a can will do that."

"It's all right... Nat," I said.

"Frank. If I could impose," said Nat.

He reached up and touched the top of his head.

"There's something stuck in my head. Could you remove it?"

"Sure." I bent over for a closer look. It was my fly. "I'm afraid this is gonna hurt some, Nat."

"Go for it, Frank."

He grunted as I worked the hook out. I removed the fly and put it back in my fly box.

"Thanks."

As I went back to stand with Jackie, he raised both his little arms above his head, stretched, yawned, and took a deep breath.

"It feels so good to be back in the fresh air."

Jackie whispered to me, "Did he just get taller?"

"Yeah... when he stretched," I whispered back.

I began to hose him off. Nat turned in a circle so I'd get every spot with the water stream. We watched in amazement as bits of plastic and every species of micro-flora and fauna swirled down the drain. He stretched again—and again, he seemed to grow taller by inches. I tossed him a clean shop towel from the shelf, and he proceeded to dry himself.

"Now what?" Jackie asked.

"I need to get you to a doctor?"

"I mean, what do we do with him?"

"Listen. Nat. I need to take Jackie to the doctor."

He nodded. "Sorry about your foot, Jackie. Hope it's not broken."

She just nodded.

"I need to close the garage door. Will you be OK for a while?" I said.

"Sure, Frank," he answered.

I grabbed a few old magazines that were going to be put out with the recycling and a water bottle and unfolded a lawn chair to put them on.

"Here's some water and something to read." Reaching into my pocket, I retrieved a Power Bar and said, "Here's something to eat." I put it on top of the magazines.

Jackie and I got into the car. I pressed the garage door remote. As it came down, we saw him sitting on a box, looking at a magazine. We looked at each other without a word and backed out. As we pulled into the urgent care parking lot, Jackie turned to me, "Did we lock the door to the house?"

Two hours later, we arrived back home—Jackie in a walking cast for a fractured bone in her foot. We held our breaths and pressed the garage door opener. He wasn't there. What we did see was the puddle of water and a large pile of wet hair on the old magazine next to which sat the meat scissors from the kitchen. A trail of water proceeded up the stairs into the house. Jackie was on the verge of combustion.

The trail took us through the kitchen into the den. There was a wet spot on the La-Z-Boy, and the remote was wet.

"At least he turned off the TV when he was done," was all I could manage.

The trail led us up to our bedroom. We slowly opened the door. From the bathroom came the merged sounds of toothbrushing and humming. Can-man had his back to us. He was now adult-size and wearing my bathrobe, pajamas, and slippers. His hair was slick, curly, shiny, and dark black; the back cut at the top of the neck. I approached the bathroom quietly. Jackie thought differently.

"Fuck this shit," she said as she stomped over and banged on the door. He stopped humming and brushing; and turned slowly to face us, toothbrush in hand like a fine brandy. My mouth jutted open. Jackie muttered, "Oh my God!"

Standing before us, in our bathroom, was none other than Mr. Boh, a.k.a. Natty Boh, the one-eyed mustachioed mascot of National Bohemian Beer and the de facto symbol of Baltimore.

"Frank. Jackie. I waited in the garage for over an hour, then decided you'd prefer to come home to see me well-groomed. I hope you'll forgive me, Frank, for wearing your clothing and for the toothbrush, whosoever it is. You'll be pleased to know that your choices in soap, shampoo, shaving cream, toothpaste, deodorant, and cologne were totally acceptable.

"Jackie, it appears from the cast that you did, in fact, break your foot on the can. May I extend my sincerest apology for any part I played in your injury. And I must say that you look stunning in an eye patch. I have always been partial to one-eyed women. I considered wearing a patch myself, but the ad people thought it would put forth the wrong image. What can you do? I'm at the mercy of those who write my paycheck.

"I had a brief look in your closet, Frank, and was happily surprised to see that we wear the same size right down to our shoes. So, if you could lay out some clothing for me on the bed. White dress shirt—I prefer a spread collar—dark trousers, suspenders, sensible bowtie, boxers, and black shoes. And a sleeveless undershirt. I believe they are referred to as *wife-beaters*, a deplorable term. I prefer the English term *singlet*. Now, if you'll excuse me. I'll just finish up here. Then maybe we can sit in the living room and have a nice chat about what I'll be needing."

With this, he closed the bathroom door.

When I looked back at Jackie, I expected to see a scowl, but instead, I saw her, head tilted, smiling and primping her hair.

"Imagine that," she said. "Natty Boh in *our* home. I didn't even know he was real. While you get his clothing, I'll go downstairs and fix us a nice lunch. He must be famished."

I laid out the clothing as he had instructed, taking extra care that nothing was worn or wrinkled. Then I joined Jackie with food preparation.

"What do you think will happen next?" she asked.

"Well, I kinda saved his life. We gave him the use of our house and my clothing. In a few minutes, we'll be feeding him. He is really in our debt."

"I know. But he's a celebrity. In our house, Frank! We need to help him in any way we can. He is the living symbol of our city."

"I think after lunch, he'll probably ask for cab fare and will be off."

"Maybe he'll give us tickets to an Orioles game," she said.

As I finished setting the dining room table, I looked up, and there he was. He looked better in my clothing than I did. My wife came in with a plate of pickles, potato chips, and an assortment of drinks, including his namesake beer. He smiled and held the can to his face. We all smiled.

"Those aren't Utz chips, are they?" he asked.

"Yes, of course, they're my favorite. I have other kinds of Utz if you prefer: barbeque, Old Bay, crab—"

"No, please take them away," he said as he averted his gaze and began to sob.

"I thought you'd be fond of these. You did have a thing with the Little Utz Girl. You guys were on billboards all over town," I said.

"Frank, leave the man alone. Can't you see he doesn't want to talk about it?"

"No. I need to start facing the pain. The billboards were just a marketing campaign, but we did date for a time."

"Didn't work out?" Jackie asked.

He shook his head and added, "I broke it off. She took it real hard. It was her first serious relationship. I didn't realize she could bear such a grudge. Must have had a huge chip on her shoulder." He looked at us for a reaction. We finally got it and smiled. "She's the one who put me in the can."

"She did that?" I asked.

"How?" Jackie added

"Right after the break-up, I get a call from her. She wanted to patch things up. Says she couldn't get away from the plant. Asks me to come up to Hanover." He turned toward me and said, "You know how you think *I shouldn't do this*, but you do it anyway?"

I nodded. "We've all had experiences like that."

"Before I knew it, some thugs put a plastic bag over me and threw me into the shrink-wrap machine. The last words I heard were *Nobody fucks with the Little Utz Girl*. Once they got me small enough, they stuffed me into an old National Bohemian can to add a dash of irony. And, to top it off, they buried me in the riverbank near Monkton; that's where we had our first date."

"That vindictive bitch!" I said.

"Well, you're free now," exclaimed Jackie.

"Yes. Thanks to you good people. And I learned a lot from the experience. I now realize what I need is not a young girl, but a mature woman who is understanding and sympathetic."

He tucked the cloth napkin in his collar. "So, Jackie, if you don't mind my asking, what happened to your eye?"

"Childhood accident. Riding my bike, not paying attention, didn't see the branch."

"Ooh. That must have been painful."

"Oh yeah. You got that right. And three surgeries at Wilmer. But they weren't able to save the eye."

"Sorry to hear that. It must have been tough to deal with that as a kid."

"Yes, it was. I had a glass eye for a long time."

"They look pretty natural these days," he said.

"It looked OK, I guess."

"So, what was the problem?"

"It kept falling out, at the worst possible times."

"I see."

"Like running to first base. Like leaning over the soup bowl. Like laughing."

"Ouch!" he said empathetically.

"The patch was an improvement," she said. "It's easier to deal with the stupid pirate jokes."

"So sorry to hear that."

"Thanks, Nat. And how about you? What's the deal with your right eye?" she asked.

"Gunther's got it, right?" I said to add some levity.

"That's very funny, Frank. I haven't heard that—"

"You haven't?"

"Today!" he said.

(Gunther Beer had been the competing beer in our city back in the day. Their slogan, *Gunther's got it*, was the inside joke to explain Natty Boh's missing eye.)

He went on. "No, I was born this way. The kids didn't make fun of me."

"No?" asked Jackie.

"They were afraid of me. I wished I could have a glass eye, but where would I put it? I dropped out of school. I came to realize that I could overcome my deficit by being suave. People can overlook just about anything if you're cool."

I saw Jackie nodding and smiling as she stood to get the food. Nat hadn't opened his can of Natty Boh.

"Would you prefer something else to drink? I just thought you'd like—"

"Please. Do you have any imported beers? A Belgian, perhaps?"

"We have Guinness," I said.

"I'll have a Guinness then, if you please," he said.

"Sure, Nat," Jackie said.

"Me too, hon," I said.

"Get it yourself."

She returned with Nat's Guinness and a tray of sandwiches.

"Everything's delicious," he said. "I really appreciate your hospitality," smiling for a long time at Jackie, then briefly at me.

Jackie looked up at Nat and asked, "Nat, are you seeing anyone?"

"No."

He looked at Jackie. She looked down and smiled.

We ate the sandwiches. Jackie brought out coffee and Smith Island Cake for dessert. Nat savored every morsel.

"Frank, may I ask you a special favor?"

"Anything, Nat."

"Your grooming supplies were quite adequate except for one necessity."

"What's that, buddy?"

"Pomade. I've been using it since I started in advertising. It's the only thing that keeps my curls right on either side of my part. In fact, it's in my contract. I'm not to be seen in public unless I look just like in the ads; otherwise, I could be let go. Would you kindly procure for me some high-quality pomade? I'm partial to Dapper Dan."

"Sure, Nat. It may take a while."

As I think back, they seemed happy to see me leave.

I went to dozens of stores before I found pomade, but it wasn't the brand he wanted; that would be special order. It was hours later before I made it back home. The downstairs was empty. The table had been cleared and the dishes put away. Then I heard voices and the sound of box springs. The bedroom door was locked, but I was able to open it with my Swiss Army knife. Just before I entered, I heard Nat say, "This *is* the land of pleasant living."

He was lying on our bed, smiling, his arm around Jackie. The hairs of his naked chest were painstakingly groomed.

"Hello, Frank. Did you find the pomade?" he asked.

"… Yes."

"Dapper Dan?"

"… No. Badger. It's all they had."

"OK."

"What's going on here?" I asked.

"You mean this?" His head turned toward Jackie.

"Yes, *this*!" I said.

"Jackie and I are getting to know each other. We have so much in common. From the moment we met, I guess you could say we saw eye to eye—my left and her right."

I just stood there like an idiot.

"Frank," said Nat. "Why don't you put the Badger down on the dresser? I'll be needing it soon. Maybe there are some errands you can run."

I heaved the Badger at Nat. It struck the headboard and landed next to him. He picked it up and examined it. Then he opened it up and smelled it.

"Not bad." Then he held it under Jackie's nose. "What do you think, darling?"

She sniffed, then replied, "Nice."

"See, we're in total agreement. That's so rare these days? How much do I owe you, Frank?"

"$13.59 plus tax."

"How about I give you a twenty?"

All I could think to do was nod.

"Jackie's purse is on the floor. Why don't you take a twenty from her wallet and go."

I went to the purse and opened the wallet. I saw the driver's license photo of my wife as an attractive younger woman. I looked at the neat row of the credit cards, each in their own pocket, each with *my* family name. I removed thirty dollars and quickly put it in my pocket, then closed the wallet and dropped it back into the purse. When I turned again toward my bed, there was Jackie, her head resting contently on Nat's chest, his arm around her—just like we used to do. And she had a smile like she used to have with me. Before I left, I took out my phone and took a picture.

"For my lawyer," I said.

I ran errands I no longer cared about. When I got home, they were gone.

I filed for divorce and got everything I wanted—except my wife.

I began to date The Little Utz Girl. It was admittedly out of spite initially, but she had become quite a hot Little Utz Woman with tremendous power in the company. I honestly fell in love.

She soon became a Vice President and got me a position as Head of Quality Control. I got to eat potato chips all day—for money.

I married that Little Utz Woman.

When we get home after work, we kiss, and she guesses which flavor I tested that day. Then we make dinner and eat potato chips in front of the TV.

Within two years, we gained two little Utz Kids and a total of one hundred pounds. But to me, she's still my Little Utz Girl.

How many people are fortunate enough to get what they want in life? I am one of those people.

A wonderful family, a well-paying job, and unlimited potato chips.

And to think, I owe it all to Natty Boh.

This *is* the land of pleasant living.

Emmett, Lizzie, and the Cherry Tree

For a Black man in late nineteenth-century Baltimore County, working in the lime kilns was among the most dangerous jobs.

Lime was used everywhere. It was in high demand to restore soil ruined by a century of tobacco farming. It was used in whitewash and mortar and poured over the dead to slow decay.

Emmett and Lizzie Coates lived in a one-room cabin near the banks of the Gunpowder River. It was an easy walk to the Ferguson Lime Kiln, where Emmett and three other Blacks kept the wood fire going twenty-four hours a day. They shoveled in crude limestone and shoveled out quick lime—the quick lime being turned into the valuable and more stable hydrated lime in a process called *slaking*. Many of these kilns, essentially large wide chimneys, were built into hillsides for structural support. Ferguson was one of the smaller operations in Baltimore County, nothing like those in Cromwell Valley or the town of Texas.

Joseph Ferguson III paid Emmett nine dollars a month for work but took out five dollars for the rent of a small cabin nearby. This was not bad for a Black man in 1890.

At least that's what Emmett and Lizzie heard most Sundays at the Bazil AME Church. They gladly walked the two miles south to Foote's Hill to be with people like them—God-fearing, giving, and kind—not like the drunkards Emmett worked with six days a week.

Emmett had heard about the labor unrest at the other lime kilns. Four years ago, a worker was found dead. Emmett didn't have to be told that the work was dangerous and the pay low. He knew he could make more working at the docks in Baltimore, but then he'd have to live in the city; Lizzie would never stand for that.

And they knew how good they had it because they had known slavery. They had been freed in 1864 while in their teens. Lizzie's two children by other men had been sold off. She wanted children with Emmett, but the second birth had nearly killed her. She was told there could be no more.

Emmett and Lizzie accepted this as God's will as they did everything in their lives.

In the uncertain world in which they lived, Emmett was sure of three things. First, he loved Lizzie with all his heart and wanted to spend his life with her. Secondly, he wanted to always provide for her. He told Lizzie these two things all the time.

But the third thing, he didn't have words for. He wanted to be part of something bigger. He had a sense of that at church and when they lay under the stars. He kept that thought to himself.

Emmett worked hard in the lime kiln. Lizzie took in laundry and did housekeeping when the work was available. They had a garden that Lizzie tended with care. She raised chickens for eggs. On a truly special occasion, there would be roasted chicken. Ferguson allowed them to pick cherries from his tree near the cabin.

To Emmett and Lizzie, the cherry tree was their Garden of Eden. On warm summer evenings, after they both bathed in the river, they would lie under its magnificent branches and look up at the sky and think how lucky they were to be alive and safe. They knew innately to savor these moments. Theirs was a world filled with white folk—most of whom did not wish them well. Lizzie knew this; both her boys had been fathered by them.

Picking the perfect cherry became their favorite game. "This one is the mother tree's pride," she would say.

"Plant that seed in the sunlight there so she can see her son grow up tall and handsome," he would say.

She'd take the seed from her mouth, and they'd walk over to the spot. He'd gently part the earth and place the seed as sweetly as a mother would place her infant in the cradle. And together, they would cover it up.

And when they kissed in cherry season, they inhaled each other's fruit scent. He could look forever into her big brown eyes. And when he kissed every bit of her, he savored her softness and earthy woman fragrance. And he would admire her beautiful brown skin he believed tied his people to the earth.

The river had fish and clean water. They had church. They had some friends. They sang in the choir. They prayed. They tithed. They were happy and cherished the time they had together.

That horrible day started with a fight during breakfast. Emmett stomped out of the cabin and got to work at seven, barely on time. The burly white foreman, Judd Lowe, his face expressionless, strode up to Emmett.

"Got bad news for you, Emmett. This here kiln is shut down."

"For good, sir?"

"That's right. Startin' today."

Upon hearing this, Emmett stepped back.

"Ashland Furnace lookin' for men?"

"I hear there's no work at Ashland. Hear there may be work at Texas."

"Naw. Too far. I ain't got no horse or mule… You know, sir, I got a wife to support."

Lowe nodded. He reached into the pocket of his overalls and handed Emmett some money. "Boss told me to give you this to tide you over."

Emmett counted the money.

"Fifteen dollars."

"Now, if you don't want it, just give it back. He didn't have to give you nothin', you know."

Emmett put the money in his pocket.

"He said you can stay at the cabin as long as you can pay the rent. Boss told me to come by on the first of every month to collect."

"How can I pay for the cabin *and* my food?"

"All I know is that you people always seem to find a way."

"I know plenty of *my peoples* who ended up dead or in jail."

"There's nothing more I can do." And he started to walk away.

"Listen. Mr. Lowe, sir. I can find me a couple of boys and we can get this place runnin' again. I mean good church-goin' boys. Not them drunks I was workin' with. And we do it for less money. We'll work hard, sir."

Lowe kept walking.

"Look at me when I talk to you!" Emmett stood wide-stanced, teeth clenched behind tight lips.

Lowe stopped in his tracks and turned around. His face was flushed. Veins stuck out in his neck. Emmett could see the man's yellow jagged teeth and his fingers congealing into fists. He could hear each hissing breath as Lowe walked back toward him. Emmett knew that look, the look that came just before a whipping.

"You tellin' me what to do, boy? I seen them scars on your back. Didn't you learn nothin' from getting whipped? Guess it's up to me to educate you."

Lowe reached under his coat and pulled out a two-foot-long wooden baton, stained and worn. As he approached Emmett, he slapped his left palm with the stick, harder and harder. Emmett stood his ground. Lowe raised the baton and swung it at Emmett's head. Emmett blocked the blow with this left forearm and countered with a punch to the jaw. Lowe fell to the ground. As he got to his feet, he grabbed a handful of lime and slung it into Emmett's eyes. As Emmett screamed in pain, Lowe circled his prey, striking him on his neck, shoulders, legs. Every time Emmett tried to cover up, he exposed the foreman's next target.

"You learnin' yet, boy?" he said, followed by another blow.

"I don't think your plan is gonna work. Know why? Cause we can't use no blind coons here at the kiln."

A blow to the back of the head brought Emmett to his knees. With the next blow, Emmett fell to the ground, dead.

Lowe removed the fifteen dollars from Emmett's pocket. He dug a shallow grave, dragged Emmett into it, and shoveled piles of lime on him, making sure there was no blood to be seen. Then he went home to eat breakfast with his wife.

When Emmett didn't come home for supper, Lizzie lit the lantern and went to look for him. At midnight she returned home and cried until daybreak. She came to the kiln early the following day to find Lowe roping off the area. She saw the signs reading "CLOSED. NO TRESPASSING."

"Excuse me, sir. My husband, Emmett Coates, works here. You seen him?"

"Yeah, I seen him. Showed up for work yesterday morning drunk. We had to close the place down."

"No, sir. That can't be my Emmett. My Emmett not

a drinkin' man."

"Well, he was drunk yesterday. Can't work drunk in a lime kiln. Too dangerous as it is—even when you sober."

"Could you tell me where he is?"

"Don't know. Yesterday morning he was heading that way," he said, pointing west.

"Did he say where he was going?"

Lowe shrugged. "Probably to buy more hooch."

"I told you Emmett is not a drinkin' man!"

"That's not what I seen with my own two eyes, lady." As she turned to leave, he added, "Since this here kiln is shut down and the rent money won't be comin' out of his wages, I'll be stopping by on the first of every month to collect."

Lizzie knew what that meant, and she thanked God that one of the first things Emmett did was to put a strong lock on the door. She knew what the white man was capable of.

She headed west, stopping at every house and business, asking about her husband. She returned home at sundown, ate, and wept.

Over the next weeks, this became her routine—each day a different direction, each time coming home tired and discouraged.

Then she gave up.

She spent more time at the church and became an elder. She took in laundry, cared for the sick, cleaned—anything to bring in a few dollars. And she paid the rent by the first of every month, leaving the five dollars under a rock on the tiny rocking chair while she locked herself in the cabin, not answering Lowe's request to let him in for a *visit*.

And that was her life until September 6, 1895, when heavy rains caused the Gunpowder River to flood its banks. It washed out the covered bridge in Warren and wreaked havoc with other mill towns along the river. The rains saturated the Ferguson Lime Kiln, now overgrown with weeds, roots, and vines. Its front wall collapsed outward as the sodden ground could no longer support it. The downpour also washed away two feet of lime.

His first breaths were imperceptible. They would not have moved dust from three inches away.

He didn't know what he was or even if he was alive. He knew nothing except that he was.

What he had become was completely and totally white. What hair was left was white. Fingernails white. Tatters of eyelashes, eyebrows, the hair in his groin and under his arms—white. And not the white of white people—but the white of white chalk. Or fresh snow. Or a brand new cotton handkerchief still with the paper band. What was left of his clothing stuck to his body like a sloppy plaster job. The lime had preserved his body like the war dead in the trenches and transformed him into something in between a corpse and the living.

Roots of nearby trees, bushes, and weeds had grown into him. Through the gash in his skull and through his nose and mouth, rootlets surrounded his brain. They made their way down his gullet into his stomach. They crawled up between his legs to wrap around his private parts and up into his intestines. They competed for space with withering sinew and muscle. Fungi attached to the finest rootlets from his fingers, toes, and everywhere else. He was nourished by the roots and the fungi. His tissues no longer needed blood or a pumping heart. His heart long ago ceased beating.

Emmett's skin had become like the thick hard leather of a shoe left out in the surf of a beach—hard, suffused with tiny glistening things. The mushroom-encrusted slit between what were eyelids held two white marbles, his tongue a leather clapper in a wooden bell. His mouth like a crack in a clay jar from which tiny insects exited, his neck like a chimney pot.

Emmett remained animal at his core but with equal parts vegetable and mineral.

Each feeble wooden movement of an arm, leg, his head, or his body ripped him increasingly free of his bondage.

When he finally arose from the wet lime to stand under the bright sun, there was a vague perception of light but nothing of the warmth of the day.

A weak cough brought up plant life in the shape of his airways, followed by brownish fluid filled with particles of dark matter.

Bit by bit, he broke free of his vegetal moorings. As he managed a step, then another, his feet felt something familiar under them. Along with vague patterns of light and shadow, he sensed he was on the path home.

Lizzie was hanging up the wash as he approached the cabin. She took one look at him, screamed, and locked herself inside. She heard his plodding footsteps make their way to the door and heard a weak glancing knock.

"Go away, you ghost. I didn't do nothin' to you. Go away before I call my husband. He big and strong and will beat you."

She sang hymns and prayed, interspersed with crying.

Hours went by, and she heard nothing more from the other side of the door. She walked over to the single window and parted the printed calico curtains. She gasped as she saw a hulking white form sitting on the porch, its head in its hands. As her gaze descended, she saw the familiar loosely woven fissures on the creature's back.

"Sweet Jesus. It's Emmett. What has become of my darling Emmett?"

She slung open the door and dashed over to Emmett. She saw rootlets and leaves from every orifice. Lizzie jumped back, then approached him apprehensively.

"Can you speak, Emmett?"

From his leather lips came a hoarse gurgling whisper: "Yes."

She bent forward, holding his stony face in her hands. With each shallow breath, she smelled deep earth.

"Lizzie… Can… I… stay… here?"

Her hesitation made him sad.

"Yes," she finally said and extended her hand to help him to his feet and into the cabin. He no longer had the working man's hands she loved. These hands were heavy, hard, and full of tiny sharp things that made her own tough hands bleed. He left a trail of spotty brown drops as he entered the cabin. She bade him sit on the bench, the sturdiest thing they had.

"Thank... you."

"Can I give you something to eat, Emmett?"

"Oat... meal."

She was relieved to be able to busy herself. She presented the steaming porridge in a large bowl. He grasped it in both hands and slowly brought it to the slit of a mouth. As he poured it in, most of it dripped from his chin. Each tiny swallow was a struggle. When the bowl was tilted fully upright, he handed it back to her.

"Thank... you... I... should... like... to... lie... down."

He eased himself onto the wooden floor next to the bed they had shared for thirty years. A puddle spread around him as Lizzie changed into her nightgown and extinguished the lantern.

"Good night, Emmett."

She reached down and rested her hand on his shoulder. Touching him had once given her so much comfort, now so much unease.

"I... am... sorry... you... have... to... see... me... like... this."

"I promised to take you in sickness and in health.

You always provided for me, Emmett. Now it's my turn."

All night long, she wept, and he listened.

At sunrise, he got to his feet. "I'm… not… Emmett… no… more… I… dunno… what… I… am… Maybe… better… off… thinkin'… of… me… as… dead… I can… go… if… you… want… Lizzie."

What he remembered as crying only came out as a rattle. Lizzie put her arms around him. He carefully tried to embrace her, feeling only a vague softness. She felt and breathed in his stony dampness.

"If… I… stay… I… gotta… support… you… some… way."

"How can you do that in your state, Emmett?"

They continued their embrace. Lizzie prayed for help. Emmett listened and followed her *amens*.

"When… is… rent… Lizzie?

"In two days."

"You… got… the… money?"

"… No. I got three dollars from cleanin'."

"I… got… fif… teen… dollar… in… my… pocket."

Lizzie looked and sighed.

"Your pockets is gone, Emmett."

"What… you… gonna… do… Lizzie?"

She stepped back from him, looked down, and said in a low voice, "… been thinkin' about leavin' the door open."

His arms dropped to his sides. He backed away from her, made his way to the large puddle next to the cabin, and lay down in it. That evening she came out to see him.

"Ain't got no choice, Emmett. Can't afford not havin' no roof over my head. I love this little place. I wanna die here."

Then she went back inside.

Two days later, Emmett, lying outside, heard a familiar heavy plodding on the cabin steps.

"I see you ain't left but three dollars," said Lowe.

"That's all I got this month, sir," said Lizzie.

"Boss needs his rent. What do you want me to do? Put you out?"

"No, sir. I try to get you the money. Could you give me more time?"

Emmett got to his feet.

"If you ain't got the money, I gotta take it out in kind."

Lowe walked toward her. She backed up until she fell back on the bed.

She shouted, "Emmett! Emmett! Help me."

"Emmett? What you callin' him for?"

Emmett Coates stood in the doorway, blocking out the sunlight. Lowe whipped around and gasped. Emmett came forward. Lowe looked into his white marble eyes, saw the slit of his mouth dripping brown, and saw the roots and vines coming from his nose and ears. He reached for his baton and struck Emmett repeatedly in the head until the rod splintered in his hand. Emmett pinned him against the wall and wrapped his stony arms around him. Lowe screamed out.

"Emmett. I didn't mean to kill you. It was an accident."

"What?" said Lizzie.

From Emmett's mouth sputtered: "No… accident."

"Lizzie and you don't have to pay no rent no more."

Lizzie cried out. "What about the boss man?"

Lowe paused. Emmett squeezed until Lowe screamed as his ribs snapped. "Boss… dead… four… months."

"So you been keepin' the money for yourself, then?" asked Lizzie.

"Times… been… hard."

Emmett squeezed harder. More screams. More snapping.

"Don't kill him, Emmett."

Emmett did not stop.

"EMMETT! THOU SHALT NOT KILL!" she screamed.

"An… eye… for… an… eye," came the gravely whisper as he continued to squeeze.

Blood ran from Lowe's nose and mouth. Lowe's last cough spewed blood into Emmett's face. Emmett tasted iron and squeezed harder. When Lowe went limp, Emmett let him drop to the floor. Lizzie was sobbing.

"Lizzie… Find… his… wallet."

She did as she was told.

"I got it."

"How… much… money?"

"Thirty-two dollars."

"Take... out... twenty... Put... the... wallet... back... in... his ... pocket."

Emmett heard Lizzie walk over to the washbasin then felt her clean his face with a cloth.

"You can't have that evil man's blood on your face, Emmett."

"Thank... you... Lizzie.

Emmett grabbed Lowe by the hair and dragged him out of the cabin, with Lizzie walking silently behind. When he heard the loud rushing of the river, he asked, "Am... I... at... the... bank... yet?"

"Emmett, it's not safe for you to go any farther. I'll do it."

Lizzie surveyed the bank and found the place with the steepest drop. She straddled the body, grabbing it by the belt and collar. With each stride, she lifted, dragged, and dropped it until she got to the right spot. Then she kneeled behind it and rolled it off the ledge. There was a loud splash. It disappeared for a moment, then rose to the surface and was carried south in the swift current. She waited until the twisting and bobbing white shirt was out of sight, then turned to Emmett and took his hand.

"You don't drink, do you, Emmett?"

"No... ma'am."

"So, that evil man was lying."

"Yes... ma'am."

"Let's go home."

The next two days brought peace for Emmett and

Lizzie. They adjusted to their new reality and were content. Emmett spent most of his days lying in the muddy riverbanks or in the standing water near the cabin.

Emmett was the first to be aware they had company from the vibrations in the ground. He sat up when he heard the two men step down from a wagon and walk up to the cabin door. They knocked, and Lizzie answered. He heard the mumbling of conversation then heard Lizzie scream: "Oh Lord, help me."

She escorted the men to where Emmett sat. At first sight of Emmett, they gasped and jumped back, covering their mouths. One said, "Jesus!" Then they looked at each other.

"Emmett. These men are from the sheriff's office."

They introduced themselves.

"Mr. Lowe's body washed up down the river," Lizzie said.

The older man stepped forward. "His wife identified the body and told us that on Tuesday morning, he said he was coming here to collect the rent. The doctor who examined the body said he'd been beat up."

"I had to tell them the truth," Lizzie cried out.

"We're taking you in for murder, Mr. Coates."

"All... right... then."

Emmett slowly got to his feet, and they shackled him. The older man said to Lizzie, "I'll send one of my men here to let you know about the trial. It will likely be this week."

They led him to the wagon; he sat in the back, and

they rode off.

In his cell, Emmett wanted only water to drink and asked that his thin blanket be wetted. The sheriff allowed Lizzie to trim the vegetation to make him as presentable as possible. A member of the church found Emmett an oversized suit.

The trial was at 9:30 AM that Friday at the county courthouse in Towson. Emmett met his lawyer for the first time at 9:00 and was told just to tell the truth and hope for the court's mercy. The trial was attended by Lizzie, some members of her church, and many whites. Lowe's wife, an old dishrag of a woman with missing teeth, scowled at Emmett throughout the proceedings. Lizzie was allowed to sit with her husband to act as his interpreter.

They heard about what Lowe had done to Emmett and that he would have raped Lizzie if Emmett hadn't stopped him. Emmett even turned to the jury and asked, through Lizzie, "If a man was about to rape your wife, wouldn't you have done the same thing?"

There were a few moist eyes among the all-white jury, but everyone in the room knew what verdict would come from the foreman. Emmett was found guilty and was to be hanged the following Monday. The judge glanced at Emmett's lawyer, who gave an almost imperceptible shake of the head, then looked down. There would be no appeal.

The Black folk cried and consoled each other. Lizzie's eyes met Mrs. Lowe's. Mrs. Lowe grinned as she left the courthouse with her family.

The hanging drew a considerable crowd. People took off from work. There were photographers and reporters, even one from the Baltimore Sun.

As Emmett was led up the scaffold steps, his wrists tied behind him, a murmur arose from the crowd. Fingers pointed. There was a shout of "Hang that white coon," followed by titters.

The sheriff asked, "You wanna say something?" The crowd hushed and craned to hear.

"No... sir," he whispered.

"You wanna hood?"

"What... for?"

"So you don't have to see nothin'."

" I... can't... see... nothin'... no... how."

The sheriff signaled for the reverend from the Bazil AME Church, who stepped up and read from the Bible, then put his hand on Emmett's shoulder.

"Thank... you... Reverend."

The reverend returned to his congregants and faced Lizzie. He held her head down tightly against his chest so she wouldn't see. She heard the trap door clank open and the collective gasp from the crowd. Lizzie broke free and cried "Emmett" as she saw him hanging beneath the gallows, his feet inches above the ground. His eye slits were open, his marble eyes staring at the crowd. She saw faint twitching movements in his arms and legs, not like the violent jerking of the one person she'd seen hanged, a slave.

The sheriff motioned for the doctor. He listened intently for a heartbeat all the time, watching Emmett's movements. "Tell them people to pipe down. I can't hear nothin'."

The sheriff turned to the crowd and shouted, "Everybody shut up. The doctor can't hear with all your carryin' on."

From the crowd came: "Don't bother. That coon's dead. Let us at 'im."

The sheriff pulled out his pistol and fired a shot into the air. "Shut up. Everybody. Or I'll start arrestin'."

The doctor went back to listening. "I don't hear no heartbeat." He took a step back and removed the stethoscope from his ears. "I pronounce this man dead."

"What's all that twitchin'?" the sheriff whispered.

"Involuntary movements. Don't mean nothin'. It would have been more usual if he weren't in such a… petrified state."

"All right then," the sheriff said. "It's over," he called out to the crowd; they started to disperse. A few came up with knives. "No souvenirs. This ain't no lynchin'. Now go home!"

The sheriff told his deputy, "Cut him down."

The deputy reached above Emmett's head with a large hunting knife and cut through the rope. Emmett's feet hit the ground. Instead of falling in a heap, he staggered to get his footing then stood there.

Those around him also just stood there, mouths agape.

Lizzie ran up to Emmett. "Cut his hands free," Lizzie shouted to the deputy, who quickly complied. The rope fell to the ground. Emmett brought his arms in front of him and rubbed his wrists. He leaned in the direction of Lizzie's voice.

"What I suppose to do now?" Emmett whispered.

Lizzie put her arms around him.

"Don't nobody move!" the sheriff shouted. "You, go get the judge. Where's the doctor?"

"Doctor's buggy is gone. No way to know where he rode off to makin' calls," said someone.

Everyone stood there until the deputy came back with the judge, both out of breath. The judge, almost nose to nose with Emmett, said, "Hey, weren't you supposed to be hanged?"

"Yes, sir. I was."

"But you ain't dead!"

"Well, sir. I would agree, but I ain't no doctor—"

Lizzie's face lit up.

"The doctor pronounced him dead not five minutes ago," said the sheriff.

"Where's the doctor?" asked the judge.

"He's gone," said the same person who said it before.

The judge rubbed his chin. "Well, he was tried in a court of law, found guilty by a jury, and sentenced by me to death by hanging. He was duly hanged as prescribed by law and pronounced dead by a licensed doctor... The business of the court is done!"

Lizzie and her congregation jumped up and down

and praised everything they could think of. She thought she saw a smile come and go on Emmett's leathery face.

"You heard the judge, Emmett. You a free man," said the reverend.

"What do I do now?"

Lizzie faced him and held his shoulders. "Emmett, you able to talk normal now."

"Hmm. I guess that jolt done shook somethin' loose."

"Well, I'll be danged," said the judge. "Just when I thought I seen everything. A therapeutic hangin'!" and walked off shaking his head.

"What am I gonna do for work, Lizzie? How am I gonna support you?"

From the crowd came a voice. "Maybe I can help in that regard."

Walking forward, parting the crowd, was a squat, middle-aged man in a three-piece suit, ascot, bowler hat, and bushy mustache.

"My name's Simms. Adolphus Simms."

He extended his hand to Emmett and Lizzie, who shook it.

"You may have heard of my circus, The Maloney and Simms Traveling Circus. We've just been outside town for the last week and are pulling up stakes as we speak. I came into town to buy a few things and came across this crowd. I wondered what all the commotion was and was shocked to learn it was a public hanging. Good God, I thought. What a terrible thing! Larger crowds than I've had for the big top. I was already here, so I stuck around. Glad it turned out hunky-dory for you, sir. I don't know what your condition is. You can tell me all about that at a later date—"

"Stop," said Emmett. "What do you want?"

"Why, I want you to be in my show."

"As a freak?" Lizzie said.

"No, we never use that odious word—as an *oddity*, among others. You would get to travel, see things, meet people."

"How much do you pay?" asked Emmett.

"I'd start you at twenty dollars a month."

"Would I get to see him?" asked Lizzie.

"Every time we come through, three times a year."

Lizzie hugged Emmett. Emmett nodded.

"OK," he said.

"Ma'am, better say your goodbyes now. We've got to get going."

"You gonna be all right, Emmett?" asked Lizzie.

"I be fine. Twenty dollar a month good, ain't it, Lizzie?"

"Real good, Emmett. Real good."

Emmett hugged and shook hands with the church members, then got into the wagon with Adolphus. They talked.

"What are your special needs, Emmett?"

"What do you mean, sir?"

"Well, for example, what do you like to eat? And you don't have to say 'sir' to me."

"Soups mostly. Salty."

"Where do you want to live? In a tent, in a wagon?"

"Anywhere damp. I like damp."

"Do you smoke or drink?"

"No, sir, I don't."

On the ride to the circus, Adolphus told his jokes, and when each joke was over, Emmett laughed. Two times Adolphus gave Emmett's arm a little punch.

Mr. Simms was true to his word. Emmett found the circus people to be different. They treated him with unusual kindness. Even though Mr. Simms called them *oddities*, Emmett knew he was part of what everyone else called a freak show.

After a week, he could recite the patter by heart: "Come one. Come all. See the amazing Three-Thirds Man. Is he animal? Is he mineral? Is he vegetable? He's all three. Found in a lime pit and given up for dead, he miraculously came to life after being buried for two years."

As opposed to the pitches about the other sideshow attractions, what was said about Emmett was largely true.

Olga, The Bearded Lady, was no lady at all but the very hirsute Buck Johnson in a dress, falsies, and falsetto.

Chief Mugamba, The Pygmy King of the Congo, was a dwarf named Ezra Cotton from outside Philadelphia.

Mr. Singh, The Sword-Swallower from Bombay, was one turbaned Avrum Cohen who joined the circus to escape being sent to yeshiva. Some days he doubled as

Moolah, The Snake Charmer.

Otis, The Fattest Man in America, was indeed fat and ate like a horse, but if he ate the amounts listed on his billing, his food bill would have driven the circus into bankruptcy.

Mamkal, The Rubber Man from Turkey, was an unfortunate Minnesotan named Osterholm with a congenital condition that made him exceedingly double-jointed.

And, at various times, there was an Alligator Man, a Bird Man, The Human Pretzel (Osterholm's cousin), and a Fire Eater.

And, to Emmett's delight, the barker would also refer to him variously as The Marble Man, The Living Fossil, The Living Statue, or The Petrified Man. Having a total of five titles made him feel important.

Emmett was allowed to let his vegetal outcroppings grow. Over time, his plant side expanded, modestly, at the expense of his mineral side. He became a little greener from deposits of chlorophyll, his stony exterior taking on a hint of the patina of a bronze statue. The mineral deposits receded enough to allow improved mobility. There was some sensation now in his fingertips and movement in his face. He was sure he was able to smile a little. His speech improved as his tongue and lips regained some plasticity. His eyeballs went from billiard ball to agate, with increasing light getting through, especially on sunny days.

More and more, the barker introduced him as The

Living Statue. He liked the *living* part of the name; it made him feel more like everyone else.

Emmett himself suggested to Mr. Simms that his act should be him standing perfectly still like a statue holding a prop. Avrum lent Emmett a sword. Christina, the trapeze artist, twisted the vines from his head to form a laurel crown and Otis' shirt became a toga. After the audience began to murmur, he would move an arm or leg or his head—to their surprise and delight.

For the first time in his life, he could speak freely to everyone. The whites thought he was white; the Black folk knew he was one of them. He delighted in talking to the children and answering their many questions even though the answer was usually *I dunno*. All these things Emmett considered blessings. And the biggest blessing of all was that no one, not even a single one of the whites who stared at him, called him bad names.

Per Emmett's instructions, Mr. Simms sent Emmett's pay to Lizzie, in care of The Bazil AME Church. With the help of a church member, she wrote Emmett, and he wrote her with the help of Mr. Singh/Cohen. And she saw him three times a year when the circus came to town. They spent hours catching up.

Emmett was liked by all. Mr. Simms especially liked him for eating as little as Otis ate a lot—he required almost no food. Emmett didn't take up valuable wagon space and was content to sleep anywhere that was damp. He found animal urine particularly invigorating; there was no shortage of that on the circus grounds.

Riverbanks remained his favorite, though, and there were often those near the circus encampments. Emmett became the most popular oddity. His salary steadily increased over the years, all going to Lizzie, enabling her to purchase the cabin and three acres around it. The cherry tree became theirs.

In the spring of 1918, The Spanish Flu took advantage of the concentrated populations of the Great War and spread in waves throughout the world. Baltimore was not spared; thousands died.

The circus lost its ringmaster, a trapeze artist, a clown, and Otis, Emmett's fat friend.

Adolphus Simms and his partners were forced to close. Adolphus had always felt his responsibility to those who made his livelihood possible. He gave severance pay and arranged for everyone's transportation home. There was a somber going-away party that served as a memorial to those who had passed away. All the equipment was put in storage and was not seen again until it was auctioned off to collectors of circus memorabilia eleven years later.

Lizzie was thrilled to see Emmett back home. She had made improvements to their little place and had put away enough money for their future.

Emmett's days were spent lying beside Lizzie or buried in the riverbank with Lizzie sitting just above him, massaging his back with her heels, singing hymns from church, and talking to him. In the summer, they would eat cherries; that is, Lizzie would eat them. For Emmett, she would squeeze the juice into his mouth, giving him a hint of what he had experienced before. It was good enough.

One beautiful June day in 1920, Lizzie called out to Emmett that she had found the most beautiful and perfect cherry she had ever seen, and was saving it in her apron for him. He waved at her from the river. Laughing, she skipped back into the cabin.

When he was finished bathing, Emmett slowly made his way up the muddy bank and sat on its edge where they always sat—where she liked to sing and talk to him. He waited for her until he sensed the fading of the day. Then he remembered something. While he was in the river, his head underwater, there was a sound. It was faint and rough as all sounds were to him. As soon as his head broke the surface, he saw the moving shadow overhead that he knew was a hawk. He thought nothing more of it until this moment. Something wasn't right. He made his way to the cabin, feeling the dread well up within him.

"Lizzie. Lizzie."

He threw open the door. Silence.

There was an emptiness that he had forgotten since his days as a slave. He again called her name. He took tiny shuffling steps at first, then dropped to his knees and crawled and felt.

When his hand touched her still leg, he stopped and got to his feet. He bent over, picked her up, and laid her on the bed. He knelt beside her and wept until he knew the night had come. Among the soft, hoarse cries and dry tears, he undressed her.

He caressed her hair—hair he knew by now would be grey—and how it would look against her chocolate skin. He had thought many times how beautiful that looked, and when Lizzie would be old, how beautiful she would look in that different kind of way. He felt white people, for all their advantages in life did not age as well as coloreds, and, to Emmett's way of thinking, this was a gift of God. He knew God was ageless, and this made his own people more in God's image than the whites. That was a thought he kept to himself.

He caressed her body and thought he once again felt her softness. As he kissed her fingers, he thought he smelled their cooking. As he kissed her lips, he thought he heard their songs. And as he kissed her body, he thought he smelled its fragrance.

He found her apron and searched in the pocket until he reached her prize. It was the largest cherry. In his mind, he saw its deep redness and tasted its sweetness.

He gently spread her thighs and placed the fruit in the place where only he was trusted to be.

Then he carried Lizzie her to the bank.

He went to where he liked to bury himself, and he dug. He placed her deep into the space. Then he crawled in and put his arms around her, drawing her nearer and nearer until their lips touched.

He felt the cool mud from the bank collapse around them. Then he closed his agate eyes.

Rootlets from his mouth found her mouth, and the tiny filaments from his fingertips found hers. Roots replaced sinews, vessels, nerves. The connections brought Emmett ever closer to Lizzie.

And the fungi connected them to the subterranean world of whispers.

He brought her into his world, and she was welcomed.

Emmett and Lizzie came to know which trees were suffering and which were faring well. And to those suffering, they sent nutrition. And the underground web of life embraced Emmett and Lizzie by sending nourishment to the seed within her.

All the sadness they knew on the earth was forgotten, overshadowed by the joy they knew within each other's arms and of being part of something grand.

And the seed, their child, grew.

From their love

And from their very flesh

Their seed grew into the most beautiful cherry tree in Baltimore County.

Acknowledgments

Many people generously offered their time to help me make these better stories.

My sincere thanks to those who provided feedback on one or more stories: Eileen Stang, my wife; David and Elissa Kaplan; C. Fraser Smith; Ed Greenhood; Rich and Linda Cooper; Jane Cimino; Phil Cohen; Betsy Gamberg; Steve Stern; Shira Kramer; Howard and Jill Stang; Henryk Grynberg; Mike Watriss; and John Shields. And from Apprentice House Press—Tyler Zorn, student editor, and Kevin Atticks DCD, Director.

A special thanks to the Research Library at the Historical Society of Baltimore County for painstakingly answering my historical questions.

My gratitude to Karen Miller, the Library Manager of Oldfields School, and Joan Carter, '81, Former Director of Alumnae Affairs of Oldfields School, for providing details about the school and its most famous alumna, Wallis Warfield, a.k.a. The Duchess of Windsor.

And finally, thanks to Rachel Moulton, my editor.

About the Author

Michael Stang has written over forty plays, many of which have been produced in the U.S. and Australia.

His love of the short story began in grade school and was rekindled during Covid when this collection was written.

Dr. Stang is a retired emergency physician who came to Baltimore for his residency and remained. Besides writing, he enjoys travel, biking, fly fishing, and woodworking.

He lives in Baltimore with his wife.

Apprentice House Press
Loyola University Maryland

Apprentice House is the country's only campus-based, student-staffed book publishing company. Directed by professors and industry professionals, it is a nonprofit activity of the Communication Department at Loyola University Maryland.

Using state-of-the-art technology and an experiential learning model of education, Apprentice House publishes books in untraditional ways. This dual responsibility as publishers and educators creates an unprecedented collaborative environment among faculty and students, while teaching tomorrow's editors, designers, and marketers.

Eclectic and provocative, Apprentice House titles intend to entertain as well as spark dialogue on a variety of topics. Financial contributions to sustain the press's work are welcomed. Contributions are tax deductible to the fullest extent allowed by the IRS.

To learn more about Apprentice House books or to obtain submission guidelines, please visit www.apprenticehouse.com.

Apprentice House
Communication Department
Loyola University Maryland
4501 N. Charles Street
Baltimore, MD 21210
410-617-5265
info@apprenticehouse.com • www.apprenticehouse.com

CPSIA information can be obtained
at www.ICGtesting.com
Printed in the USA
BVHW051824230522
637867BV00011B/313